Destiny

Mahlon Palmer

authorHOUSE®

AuthorHouse™
1663 Liberty Drive
Bloomington, IN 47403
www.authorhouse.com
Phone: 1 (800) 839-8640

Published by AuthorHouse   05/10/2016

ISBN: 978-1-5049-7984-9 (sc)
ISBN: 978-1-5049-7982-5 (hc)
ISBN: 978-1-5049-7985-6 (e)

Library of Congress Control Number: 2016906182

Print information available on the last page.

Any people depicted in stock imagery provided by Thinkstock are models,
and such images are being used for illustrative purposes only.
Certain stock imagery © Thinkstock.

This book is printed on acid-free paper.

Contents

KING

This pure white Border Collie puppy was born sometime in the mid 1940's and almost immediately became Dick's best friend, in fact they became nearly inseparable.

Dick named his new friend, "King" after the dog in the radio series, "Sergeant Preston of the Yukon and his dog King". When Dick left home to join the military, King nearly died from a broken heart.

Without a doubt, King was Dick's very best friend throughout his childhood, thus the reason his picture is on the front of this Book.

Introduction

On July 31, 2014 Mahlon (Dick) Palmer suffered a severe heart attack while at the Clinton Farmer's Market in Clinton, New York. The complete story regarding that event is detailed elsewhere in this book; however it is important to mention it here because that single event had a direct impact on this book's creation. You see, I Dick Palmer, spent three nights in the hospital where I became acquainted with two of the nurses on the midnight shift. Whenever they had a break they would come into my room to talk and would ask me to tell them a story about my life. On the third night, just prior to my release, they requested that I write a book about those many travels and adventures throughout my life. This book is the direct result of that request. So again, I ask the question, why did I survive this event, when I had already had the opportunity to see the "Other Side"? Was it by the Grace of God, Was it Chance or, *WAS* it *"DESTINY"*?

In addition, this book was written primarily for those young adults who are growing up in an environment, similar to the environment to the one I grew up in, where if the latest gadget or trend is not available to them, they must do without. It is also generally accepted that these same young adults, must be fortunate enough to either; win the lottery, receive a rather large gift or inheritance, or incur massive debt that will allow them to become successful in today's world. In the event they choose debt, or by necessity are forced into incurring a debt that frequently will require a lifetime to liquidate, there is another option. This book details how one young man was able to bypass all of the above stated options and turn it into a career that is the envy of many of his educated peers.

Therefore, this book proves beyond a doubt, you are only poor if you believe you are poor, thus giving you no chance for success. You *do not* need to spend a hundred thousand dollars on a super education just to have a couple of letters after your name so you LOOK important, then end up with a lifetime of debt that you may never get liquidated. For myself, I spent a total of $150 (yes, that is one hundred and fifty dollars), for collage debt and a total of ten hours in the classroom. Also remember, virtually everything you learn in college, in fact most educational settings, is designed to specifically pass the next test so you can move on to the next chapter; it does not prepare you for the real test which is called life. Also do not forget, the text book you are studying is most likely the same book your professor learned virtually everything they know. If the previous statement is true, then why not just buy the book and eliminate the huge expense called college tuition. Although I must admit my philosophy *does* eliminate all of the good time partying on campus.

Dedication

This Book is dedicated to the three women who have made the greatest difference to me throughout my life, and obviously the first person was my mother, Jewel Jordan Palmer who was responsible for laying the foundation in which everything that followed would be built upon. She was an extremely hard working person who never appeared to take a break. Each day began by going to the barn at five o'clock in the morning and helping with the milking and other chores, then returning to the house to create breakfast for the hungry mob that would follow by around seven. Breakfast was always the same, pancakes, eggs and bacon with gravy and maple syrup. The rest of her day was filled with cooking, house cleaning, baking and all the other things mothers do. In the summer she even made time to have a large garden. Her normal day ended by spending another two plus hours in the barn doing the evening milking and other chores. Somehow she even made time for her four children.

You must also keep in mind the period of time when all of this was taking place was during the 1930's and 1940's when times were exceedingly difficult.

After leaving home in 1954 to join the U.S. Air Force, Dick finally had time to meet a young lady while stationed at Griffiss AFB in Rome, New York. Her name was Joy Ann Blood and she grew up in the little town of Remsen, New York, thus Joy Ann became the second most important women in his life. They were just getting well acquainted when Dick received orders that he would be transferred to Incirlik AFB in Turkey for some period of time in excess of one year. The greatest event while in Turkey was getting those letters from home. Dick believes JoyAnn wrote every day that he was gone, thus they became very close during that time. Upon Dick's return home they were married and spent the next thirty-six years moving around the country, living in Homestead, Florida; Remsen, New York; Cherry Hill, New Jersey; Baltimore, Maryland; Colorado Springs, Colorado; and finally back to Clinton, New York; all in the pursuit of Dick's dream. Tragedy struck in 1991 when she was diagnosed with cancer and after two devastating years she finally found peace.

The third most important woman in Dick's life is Barbara Putt whom Dick met through his very close Veterinary friend. They met about a year after the loss of Dick's wife, during a very difficult period in his life. After being married for thirty six years, the loneliness was devastating. Barbara and Dick have much in common, they both are great animal lovers, they both enjoy travel and most of all just enjoy each other's company.

Chapter One

THE EARLY YEARS

On November 4th, 1936 the Merle Wilson Palmer Family, residing on the Palmer Homestead in the town of Meredith, New York was presented with their fourth and final child. This boy was ultimately named by his maternal grandmother and was given the name Mahlon Richard, a name taken from the biblical Old Testament book of Ruth. The source of the middle name of Richard is unknown; however, he has been known by his family, friends, acquiesces, business associates and virtually all others by his Nick Name of Dick. His given name of Mahlon has rarely been used except for legal documents.

The Merle Wilson Palmer family was now complete with their mother Jewel Jordan Palmer and the three older boys. Cecil Eugene, the eldest, was born on July 5, 1931, followed by a pair of twins, born on December 11, 1933; Roy Wilson being the eldest and Ronald Leo.

Merle Palmer and his family lived on the family farm, located on Palmer Hill Road in the town of Meredith, New York. The farm was originally purchased in 1911 by Leo Palmer, Dick's grandfather and remained in the Palmer family for more than one hundred years.

Farming in the 1930's during the "Great Depression" and on into the 1940's during the Second World War was a very challenging endeavor where everyone was expected to carry their share of the load, regardless of their size or age. As such, the typical workday began about 6:00 o'clock in the morning and ended near 8:00 o'clock at night, Monday through Saturday. Sundays were much different, always being considered a day of rest. Only those tasks that were absolutely necessary, such as: milking the cows, feeding the animals and cleaning the barn were done on Sunday; never gathering hay, planting crops or cutting wood was allowed. Sunday morning always ended by going to church and was always followed by a big Sunday dinner. Sunday afternoon was then free for play (if you had any energy left).

A typical week day, including Saturday, began at 06:00 A.M by milking the cows, (mostly by hand), feeding the other animals and cleaning the barn (always the barn had to be cleaned) unless if school was in session, Merle would then clean the barn after the kids had gone to school. Typically the barn gutters were cleaned by shoveling the manure onto a wagon or sleigh (depending on the weather) then taking it to the fields and spreading it on the land by hand. Horses provided the only power to pull the sleigh or wagon, so by the time a kid was seven or eight years old they were pretty competent at handling and driving a team of horses.

A typical school day was a bit different. The work day began at six A.M. by milking 25 to 30 cows by hand and was normally completed by around seven o'clock at which time Jewel would serve the standard breakfast fare which always included pancakes, creamed gravy, eggs with bacon and always homemade maple syrup. Breakfast was over by about 7:30, leaving just enough time to walk the two miles to school. School was usually over by around 3:30, followed by a walk home, sometimes cross lots just to change the scenery. Once home, depending on the weather, there were always tasks that needed to be competed such as; haying, filling silo, cutting fire wood, picking stone, etc. Supper was always served around 5:30, then back to the barn for the evening milking.

Milking was usually complete by 8:30 PM and the day's work was finally done. Did anyone ask you to go to bed? Not hardly. Bed was always a very welcome relief.

Now a very logical question would be. When did farm children of that generation have time for school work? *THEY DIDN'T.* The hard cold facts were, if you didn't get it in the class room, you just didn't get it. It is hard to comprehend that philosophy in today's world but that is just the way it was.

Throughout the twentieth century most family farms had at least one dog, whether it was a cow dog, sheep dog, guard dog or just a plain old mutt, and the Palmer farm was no different. In fact they had two dogs; one Border Collie male (herding dog) and one part Border Collie female (cow dog) used for controlling cattle. During the mid 1940's, those two dogs produced a litter of pups that were primarily Border Collie and Dick pleaded with his parents to allow him to have his own dog. After much pleading he was given permission to keep one of the pups.

The pup that Dick selected was a pure white male that had all the features of a Border Collie and weighed some fifty or sixty pounds. Dick named his new companion "King" after the dog in the radio series "Sargent Preston of the Yukon".

Dick and King immediately became inseparable. King learned to be a good cow dog, he learned to hunt, he played ball, whatever Dick did if it was physically possible King was always with him. This very close bond remained for many years until 1954 when Dick graduated from high school and joined the Air Force. That separation was very traumatic for King and nearly cost him his life.

During those difficult years many items were in very short supply, such as new clothes and toys. Virtually all clothes were hand-me-downs or just plain secondhand. Toys fell into that same category. If you were lucky enough to get a toy, new or used, you took very good care of it; however there was an alternative. If you were creative and a bit industrious you could always create/build your own toys. For example, Dick always had a fascination for guns; however he never had any real guns at that time. Thus at a very early age he built his own guns by carving them out of a piece of wood and used rubber bands for ammo. They were not dangerous, but a lot of fun. Dick also somehow acquired an old single cylinder gasoline engine that originally had been removed from a 1920/1930s washing machine. That little engine gave him many hours of pleasure in taking it apart and putting it back together, then getting it to run. Those exercises were all instrumental in helping him to learn to solve problems without the use of a book.

Dick got his first real working B B gun when he was about ten years old, a gun that assisted him in becoming an expert rifleman for the rest of his life.

During those years many necessary items were rationed and essentially became unavailable, one of those items was sugar. If you lived on a farm, as many families did, you very possibly had the option of making maple syrup for use as a substitute for sugar, thus each spring there was an added task that needed to be done.

Making maple syrup in those days was very labor intensive and required everyone to participate. For those unfamiliar with the process in those days, Dick will try to give you a brief overview of the tasks that were required. Keep in mind that making maple syrup was only done in the early springtime, frequently when the snow was still on the ground.

First the maple sap was taken from the trees by tapping the trees and hanging buckets from the tap to catch the sap.

Tapping the tree consisted of boring a new hole into the tree and driving a spiel (special pipe) into the hole and attaching the bucket to the spiel. As soon as the trees were tapped the task of gathering the sap nearly every day was required. This was a very labor intensive process and in those days was generally done by using a team of horses and a sleigh. Today's pipeline systems had not even been invented at that time. Once the sap was gathered it was necessary to 'boil it down' meaning to remove the excess water from the sap and convert it into maple syrup. This process in those days was generally done using large open pans, situated above an arch or large fireplace. The boiling process required huge amounts of dry fire wood to keep the fire burning for extended periods of time. Keep in mind this fire wood was cut with cross cut saws and split with axes and wedges.

From the time that Dick was six or seven years old he would take a kerosene lantern at about 5:30 A.M and walk to the woods, start the fires, fill the pans full of sap and then return to the barn and begin his regular days' work. The round trip walk to the woods was about three quarters of a mile.

A very similar process took place each night after milking was complete except at night the fire was 'Banked' in an attempt to keep the fire burning as long as possible during the night. It was usually

9:00 o'clock by the time Dick got back home and to bed. This routine made a very long day for a young kid.

It was always a welcome relief when Maple Syrup season was over. However each season had its own unique tasks that needed to be done after school or on weekends. In addition to making maple syrup in the early spring, spring planting was next on the list to keep the kids busy after school and on Saturdays.

The kids spring planting chores were almost exclusively restricted to 'picking stone', in other words removing any stone that could interfere with any piece of equipment. Picking stone was an extremely good way to build muscle, but very labor intensive.

Another spring job was building and/or repairing the literally miles of fence that was required to control the animals. Every foot of fence line required inspection and repair as needed. Fence repair included replacing broken fence posts, replacing or repairing all broken wires, removing any brush or new growth from along the fence as well as removing any fallen branches or trees from the fence wires.

Making hay for all of the animals was the primary additional task for the summer; however, you could and did work all day without the necessity of being bothered with taking time out to go to school. Making hay in those days was another very labor intensive task. The first step in the process was mowing the grass, using a team of horses pulling a devise generally referred to as a mowing machine or sickle bar. After the hay became sufficiently dry, it needed to be raked into windrows where it could be picked up and loaded on a hay wagon for transport to the barn. Once in the barn, it again needed to be moved into its final resting place for the winter. This process was always needed; however if the weather was rainy, several more steps were required to get the hay dry.

Keep in mind, the above mentioned tasks were all accomplished by using a team of horses; however in the early 1940's a tractor was added to the farm. That tractor was one of the first tractors that had rubber tires and was a 1939 Ford Ferguson. The tractor worked great; however gasoline was in very short supply during the early 1940's throughout the war years.

The fall season also had its unique tasks that needed to be done before winter set in. Early in the fall the silo needed to be filled with corn or other fodder for the animals. Again very labor intensive and time consuming. If all of these tasks were complete there was always the necessity to cut fire wood. Keep in mind in those days there was virtually no such thing as fuel oil, electricity, propane gas or other fuels for heating your home, so wood was the only alternative. Most homes had at least two wood stoves that barely kept the pipes from freezing. Again all of this wood was cut with a cross-cut saw with a person on each end of the saw. Then don't forget all that wood needed to be split and piled for drying. There were no chainsaws or wood splitters at that time and Dick can still remember their first chain saw that he used when he was probably ten or eleven years old, a saw that was nearly as big as he.

1954 – A year of Change

The year 1954 was without a doubt the most significant year in Dick's young life as you will see. *DESTINY* played a major role in not only shaping his life at that time, but also, had significant impacts throughout his entire life and career.

The first life changing event occurred just prior to high school graduation. Being the youngest child in the Palmer family, his father had always declared that since all of his older brothers had all graduated from high school with a Regents Diploma, then his youngest son would also have the same Diploma, even if he had to go to school until he reached the age of twenty-one.

There was however one major obstacle standing in the way of accomplishing that goal. He still had to pass a History Regents exam and as usual there had been no time to prepare, much less time to cram for the test. The fateful day was in the afternoon and promptly at the appointed time the test was passed out to all of the participants. Once the doors were locked, no one could leave the room unaccompanied.

After performing a detailed review of the material, Dick decided that taking the exam would be a total waste of his time, and considering the fact he could not leave, he further accepted the fact he would be returning next year to retake the course. Since sleep was always a precious commodity, he further decided to take a much needed nap.

DESTINY took over. He was unable to fall asleep, so in desperation to kill time he started writing because he could not leave anyway. The next day when test scores were posted, "*HE PASSED*", not by much, but still passed. Interestingly, a number of the better students' state wide did not pass, thus scores were raised on a curve and so the test was not a total failure after all. As a result of passing that Regents exam Dick graduated with his class when he was seventeen years old.

As Dick's graduation approached he had been investigating the possibility of attending a trade school to learn the field of electronics; however one Sunday morning just prior to his graduation he was approached by his mother who informed him that she and Dick's father had been discussing Dick's options. They had determined there were inadequate funds for school and they had further concluded that there would be no opportunities for him on the farm. Dick's parents suggested that maybe he should seriously consider joining some branch of the military to avoid the draft so he could join the service of his choice.

After carefully evaluating the pros and cons of the US Air Force, US Army, US Navy and the US Marines he eventually chose the US Air Force since they offered a career field in Meteorology, a science that had always fascinated him throughout his entire childhood.

The summer was spent working on the farm while waiting for an opening in the Air Force that would get him into the career field of his choice. While helping with the haying and getting his few affairs in order, he was planning the greatest, and at that point in time, the most unknown game changing event of his young life. The morning of October 14, 1954 began like hundreds of days before, bright clear blue sky, milking the cows, completing breakfast and then the changes began. He loaded the few things he could take with him into the car, which was not much, essentially a tooth brush and razor the clothes he was wearing and a couple of bucks in his pocket. Dick said good-bye to his best friend King and then his mother drove him to Oneonta to the Air Force recruiting station where he would join the other new recruits for that day. As Dick and his mother departed down the road, King gave his usual farewell greeting, little knowing he would not see his friend for at least three months. Beginning that evening, King began waiting in the road, awaiting his friend's return, and he waited there for nearly two weeks, almost starving to death and barely surviving the traffic. Eventually, he decided his friend was not coming back home and his grieving slowly diminished.

There was one other unusual event that was developing on that bright sunny morning, which was still unknown to everyone at that time. South of New York City off the coast, a major tropical storm was developing that would eventually be identified as "Hurricane Hazel". As the storm continued to develop, it progressed further inland and it continued to grow to become the largest and most severe storm to ever hit New York State. Much later in the day as you will see this storm would have a major impact on a plane load of new Air Force recruits who would be trying to reach Sampson Air Force Base after their induction during that day; however there was much left to happen yet that day during the induction process.

Chapter Two

HE'S IN THE ARMY NOW

The bus ride from Oneonta to Albany was completely uneventful. For those of you who have served in the military, you probably remember your induction well; however for the others it is somewhat of a unique experience. The first thing to happen is all potential inductees are taken into a large room and required to remove everything except their shorts. Then the fun began. A team of doctors began to prod and poke every cavity; Dick was confident it was to ensure you were not carrying any contraband, or maybe it was to verify everything was in the correct location.

At this point, *DESTINY* once again changed the course of events. While waiting for the Doctors, another Doctor approached Dick and began to take his pulse. After taking his pulse a couple of times he stepped back and with a very quizzical expression on his face asked for the assistance of a second doctor. The second doctor had the same quizzical expression, then flatly stated, "Well, he is still breathing-send him in".

Many years later, when Dick was about 35 years old he was advised that he had a major bundle branch blockage in his heart and should have never passed his induction physical. Apparently the doctors had detected a significant abnormality, but either didn't know what it was, or they were short on their quota and desperately needed another body. In either case, that event without a doubt became "*THE*

GREATEST GIFT OF HIS ENTIRE LIFE" as you will see. Without going into details, that gift also almost certainly saved his life.

Significant events were not yet over for that day. Since he had passed his physical and he had taken his oath, he was now officially in the United States Air Force for a total of eight years (four years of active duty and another four years of inactive duty for a total of an eight year commitment) and so it was now time to head for Sampson Air Force Base. The Base was located on Cayuga Lake south of Geneva, New York in the central Finger Lakes Region of New York State where he would take his Basic Training

The preferred choice of transportation was by air. Remember, earlier it was stated that the day had begun with a beautiful morning; however the weather had deteriorated dramatically throughout the day with the arrival of hurricane Hazel, one of the largest and severest storms to hit central New York in many years, if not on record. In any event Dick was going to get his first airplane ride in a DC-3 twin engine plane. The plan was to depart Albany Airport and fly direct to Sampson Air Force Base. That plan was quickly abandoned due to severe turbulence and icing that was associated with Hurricane Hazel and the flight ended by landing in Syracuse, NY. The remainder of the trip to Sampson was completed by limousine, taking all night before arriving at Sampson AFB at about five o'clock in the morning.

The limousine ride from Syracuse to Sampson went directly through the City of Geneva; however the storm got to Geneva before the bus load of new recruits. Nearly the entire night was spent in helping road crews remove the downed trees caused by the hurricane so the limousine could get the new recruits to Sampson.

Once in the barracks the new recruits were told to find a bed and get some sleep, a very welcome gesture due to the long day and night before. Sleep lasted for nearly fifteen minutes, then WELCOME to the Air Force.

The first day was unique with a very full day planned. First, everyone was rounded up and herded off to the chow hall for breakfast. As soon as breakfast was over they all went to the barber shop to get the 'cut' of their choice, basically, three passes with the clippers and you were completely bald.

The next major stop was supply. First you were measured, given underwear and a bag to send your entire personal belongings home, then told to strip and dress in your brand new government issued underwear. You could keep any personal items as long as it was a tooth bush, tooth paste, razor and shaving cream. Everything else was put in the bag and sent home. You were now ready to get your whole new wardrobe issued to you to include: shoes, fatigues, dress uniforms (both summer and winter), hats, socks, underwear, etc.

Before the first day was over you would go back to your barracks and learn where everything belonged and *PUT IT THERE*, never again to be out of place. Time permitting you would start to learn how to march and learn military vocabulary. Learning the vocabulary was really quite simple as the only two options you were allowed to use were 'YES SIR' and keeping your mouth shut. By this time your day was over and no one had to ask you to go to bed.

The next few days were very much the same, very busy, like getting your first real instructions on marching, how to respond to authority, (incidentally at that stage of your career, everyone out ranks you), learning how to properly dress yourself, etcetera.

Within the first few days all the recruits were required to declare their preferred career field. Dick had already chosen the Air Weather Service (Meteorology) as his first choice and some kind of flying as his second choice. Unfortunately, both choices presented significant problems. He was basically disqualified from any flying career due to his poor eye sight and he discovered the Air Weather Service was one of the two most difficult fields to qualify for acceptance. In any case, the Air Force administered a series of nine aptitude tests to determine your qualifications. The Air Weather Service required a minimum score of at least seven out of a possible nine on all tests. Once again *DESTINY* played a role. Against all odds Dick scored 8s or 9s on all tests, thus meeting the qualifications for his first choice of a career.

Being only seventeen years old when entering the service he was quite small when he got to Basic Training, checking in at about five foot four inches tall and weighing less than 120 pounds. As a result of having worked on the farm all his life he was hard as nails, so Basic Training was like one big vacation. During the three months he was there he grew a couple of inches and gained over fifteen pounds.

There was one other type of day that was always a lot of fun. It was affectionately referred to as "get your shots day". The Air Force was always very careful to keep those days a big secret. The day would begin just like any other with marching, calisthenics, questions and answers, etc. Then it would be announced that we were going to go for a little run. After running for a mile or so we would come to a very special building, *"THE GET YOUR SHOTS"* building.

This building was not much different on the outside from all the other buildings; it was on the inside where all the fun took place. Let me try to describe the inside. It was basically one large room, divided into two sections by a three foot high partition. One section represented about two-thirds of the room with the other one third being a kind of stand-around area. Incidentally there were no chairs in the building, at least not for the GI's.

It was now time for all the troops to move inside. The instructions were; strip to the waist and form a single continuous line in the larger section. Dick forgot to mention that the partition had a gate, just large enough for one man to pass through at a time, with a medic positioned on each side. Each medic had a hypodermic needle in each hand, just waiting for the line to begin to move. The moment you stepped between the medics you received all four shots simultaneously, and then you could put your cloths back on and wait for your friends.

Suddenly a rather large fellow near the middle of the line called to the Doctor to advise him he was not feeling well and needed to get outside to get some air. The Doctor advised him he could come to the head of the line and go outside to get the needed air. The instant he hit the gate, BAM, he got all four shots and then immediately collapsed in a big pile right in front of the gate. He received a standing "O" for his performance.

There were no more significant events that occurred during the remainder of Basic Training. Each day was pretty much the same as the day before. There was always marching, to and from all meals. Every day included some type of classroom work, such as studying the history of the Air Force, studying and learning the hierarchy of the military, and how to address your superiors. There were visits to the range where shooting was always a good time, spending half of a day learning all about going in and out of the gas chamber and occasionally a trip to the swimming pool.

Time passed very quickly through the holiday season with just getting Thanksgiving Day and Christmas Day off. Guys with family close by could spend time with them, on base; otherwise the Air Force provided a great holiday meal for everyone else.

With the holidays over, the troops were now beginning to think about their next assignment. By the end of January all the troops were planning a couple of days with family, and for Dick he would spend three or four days at home then catch a bus to Chanute AFB near Champaign, Illinois where he would begin Air Weather School.

Before departing for Chanute Dick would stop at home for three or four days. It did not take King long to figure out that his friend and master had returned and as soon as they could get together it was just like the old days. They went shooting, played ball, went for walks and just spent as much time together as possible.

The three days passed quickly and it was time to leave again. This separation would last nearly five months and King was again very depressed, but not nearly as bad as the first separation.

Dick arrived at Chanute around the first of February, checked in at Headquarters, got assigned to his squadron and barracks, assigned to a bed, issued his bedding and met all of his new classmates.

His class did not begin for over a month or six weeks after he arrived at Chanute or actually the latter part of March or early April, so during that time after he arrived the Air Force kept him and the rest of the troops occupied with 'busy' work and plenty of KP (Kitchen Police) or kitchen duty.

A normal day of KP began at about 0300 hours (3:00 AM) with pealing the potatoes for the noon meal. Keep in mind there were tens of thousands of troops on the base, therefore it took a lot of potatoes. By the time the potatoes were pealed it was now time to begin washing the breakfast dishes (or should we say breakfast trays), then if all was going well you would still have time to scrub down the kitchen. By this time you were ready to eat lunch and call it a day. You generally had to walk home (back to the barracks) meaning you didn't have to march.

Non KP days could be most anything from shoveling dirt, operating jack hammers, to picking up trash and policing the area, or just about anything to keep you busy.

Finally, all the troops that would be attending Weather School had arrived and gotten settled into the routine. There were a total of 187 men that started the class. One thing Dick found very interesting was the fact that most of his classmates were college graduates; therefore they were on average about four or more years older than him.

One day was about the same as the day before, out of bed at 0430 hours or before, shave, and shower, get dressed in your fatigues and then march as a group to the chow hall for breakfast. With breakfast over it was time to march about a mile to school, rain or shine.

Weather school was very intense with 4-5 hours of class room lectures each day, followed by testing to determine how much you remembered from the previous few days' work. During the first day of class students were *emphatically* told if you were serious about graduating from Weather School then you needed to plan on spending an additional two to three hours of dedicated study time each day, plus several more hours each weekend. Apparently, many of the students did not believe that such dedication was required because each Monday morning there would be a few new empty beds in the barracks. It was Dick's belief that since a very high percentage of the students were already college graduates, many believed they could coast through this course like they did in college. They were in for a very rude awaking since the average dropout rate throughout the course was approximately 40%. Another major difference in the military where many decisions have life and death consequences, a second chance is very rare. One thing that always appeared odd was that those highly rated students that 'washed out' of the school were almost always reassigned to much less demanding careers. During the first week or so Dick had a very difficult time with studying and completing homework, since if you remember he had never had time for homework as a kid in grades 1 through 12 due to work on the farm. He quickly adjusted however to the new regimen.

With being so busy, time passed quickly and graduation was fast approaching near the end of August. On the last day of class they took all graduating students into a large room to find out where their first duty assignment would be. There were 78 graduating students and there were 78 duty stations posted on the board, then they started reading the names of each student in descending order by final grade. As they read your name you got to choose any station remaining on the board, then that station was removed. Dick was 43rd and selected Griffiss AFB in Rome, NY. As a note of interest there were 187 students at the start of the class.

The next day or two was spent cleaning the area, packing bags and making reservations for a departure as quickly as possible. Dick took the bus back to Oneonta, then back to the farm in Meridale, NY.

Once again his old friend King was overjoyed to see his master. This stay would only be for two or three days; however the visits would be much more frequent since Griffiss AFB was only about one hundred miles away.

It was now time to make his way to Griffiss AFB and get checked into his new Duty Station. What a surprise this would be. The first person he met was his new Commanding Officer, a Major, and a person he would gain a great deal of respect for over the next ten to twelve months.

The next person he met was his new First Sergeant, a fellow I will refer to as John. John was much older than Dick by nearly ten years and they almost instantly became close lifelong friends, staying in touch until John's death around 2010. John and his family lived in Ohio and over the years they visited a number of times. When Dick and John had time off at the same time John would travel to the farm with Dick as traveling to Ohio was much too far for a weekend.

It was now time for the biggest surprise of his new assignment. When they went to the barracks to get 'settled in' Dick discovered he would have a private room, virtually no work details, no KP, and a permanent Class 'A' Pass (meaning he could go on and off base at will). Why you may ask!

There were a number of reasons: One being due to the criticality of their mission, they constantly worked rotating shifts since qualified personnel were generally very scarce (refer back to the failure rate in

Mahlon Palmer

class dropouts). He further discovered this policy was worldwide since there were few alternatives.

You may wonder what was so critical about the weather station. First, most weather stations were located where there was significant flying activity, as was the case at Griffiss. Griffiss AFB was a part of the Air Defense Command and had two large fighter squadrons assigned; one squadron of F-94 jets and another squadron of F-89 all-weather interceptor jets.

Therefore, the primary mission of this weather station, as well as most others, was to support the flying activities and a close second was to provide critical weather information nationwide and worldwide in support of weather forecasting and analysis.

The Weather Station at Griffiss AFB was very typical of hundreds of weather stations around the country and around the world particularly where there was flying activity.

A typical weather station generally consists of two parts; the observation section and the forecasting section.

The observation section generally provides the following functions;

Observing and reporting ANY and ALL changes in the weather conditions such as:

Changes in precipitation type, as well as intensity.

Changes in visibility and the reasons for those changes.

Changes in ceilings (defined as cloud bases that cover 60% of the sky) to include cloud types (27 distinct types) as well as height of tops and bases of each layer

Significant changes in barometric pressure

Significant changes in wind direction and intensity, with particular attention to major wind shifts (usually an indicator of a frontal passage).

The absence or presence of certain types of clouds such as cumulonimbus (thunderstorms); and/or the presence of virga that will give an indication of severe down drafts which are a couple of examples of unusual conditions.

Any unusual phenomenon that would present a hazard to flying was recorded and reported

Once a qualifying event occurred it must immediately be distributed to any and all parties concerned, both locally and nationally. National notification was done by teletype.

Each hour a standard observation was required that was recorded and transmitted by teletype around the world, then each six hours a much more complete observation was taken and distributed. That observation included all the above information, plus much more information that was necessary to produce all the charts that were used in forecasting the weather. This complete information was also used in briefing pilots and air crews that were flying around the world. The six hourly reports additionally included information regarding precipitation types and amounts, etc.

Another major task for observers was plotting weather information on to appropriate charts and graphs that was received from around the world via teletype. Those were then analyzed by forecasters prior to preparation of weather forecasts and pilot briefings.

As a note of interest, those charts were plotted and analyzed every six hours and would take a good plotter two to three hours of effort each time they were prepared.

As a further note of interest, all the charts that you see today on the WEATHER CHANNEL, are all produced and analyzed by computer, basically without the assistance of the human hand. We've come a long way since the '50s.

The Forecasters of yesteryear were much different than what is seen today. For example, 50-60 years ago there was virtually NO radar, as contrasted to today where weather radar is everywhere and does not require extensive training to use it. With today's RADAR you can view the entire North American continent that depicts every possible weather phenomenon at a glance. Then you can supplement all of that data with satellite imagery of the world.

After viewing all the weather on your computer, you then can consult numerous computer generated weather forecasting models, compare many opinions, and then choose your favorite. In fact, with virtually no training most anyone can consult their telephone or laptop computer and arrive at a fairly accurate twelve hour prognostication.

As stated earlier, there were two main components to a weather station; the observation group and the forecasting group.

Weather observers were generally those individuals serving their first enlistment in the Air Force and usually held a rank of Staff Sargent or lower and would have had to successfully complete Air Weather School.

On the other hand Weather Forecasters generally held higher ranks due to the extensive training that was required. Many times they were college graduates and had received their commission through ROTC. In either case they were frequently career oriented.

While stationed at Griffiss, Dick had an opportunity to do quite a bit of flying with his commanding officer the Major who had been a pilot in Korea and flew frequently to maintain his currency, thus he often invited Dick to go along. Flying with him was always in a C-45 small twin engine passenger plane. Since the Weather Station was closely associated with the F-94 Fighter Squadron, Weather personal could frequently catch a joy ride on one of those. Those rides were always quite a hoot since if the pilots could get you sick, the flight was considered a success. If you did get sick your first task when you got back was to clean up the airplane and more importantly your helmet.

Also while stationed at Griffiss, Dick met a young lady named Joy Ann Blood who one day would become his wife.

In the fall of 1956 Dick received his orders for an overseas assignment, an assignment so classified they didn't know where to send him except to Manhattan Beach AF Station. There were a total of four airmen from around the country on those orders.

After a few days leave (vacation in civilian talk) it was time to pack the suitcase and head for the bus station and then on to Manhattan Beach Air Force Station in NY City; however before leaving there was one remaining task. As in the past Dick had to say goodbye to his longtime friend King, but this goodbye was different. Dick did not know it at the time but he would never see his friend again as King would die during the coming year. There were many dogs throughout the years after King, many better trained than King, but he was the first and the one that left the greatest impression.

After arriving at Manhattan Beach he met the other four airmen listed on the orders and they began preparing for their journey to somewhere. There were now four guys who had no idea where they were headed, so in desperation to send them someplace, the powers to be decided to send them to Frankfurt Germany and let them determine where to send them from there.

Once in Frankfurt, it took another three days to make a decision on where to send them. During those three days, the four guys had an opportunity to see much of Frankfurt; the only requirement was they had to check in each morning to see if any decisions had been made about their final destination. While travelling around Frankfurt, Dick found and purchased his first good 35mm camera. The camera was a Kodak Retina 3c. In 1956 it was considered top of the line however by today's standards it is considered an antique. In any case that camera has travelled many thousands of miles and has taken literally thousands of photos.

In desperation to do something, the powers to be decided to send the four guys to Athens, Greece to let them figure out the next move. From this point on all travel would be in military cargo planes, generally of the C-119 Cargo type. The C-119 Cargo plane was very unique, in that it was designed to carry large, heavy cargo and was used for carrying personnel only as a last resort. In the next few pages an attempt will be made to describe what it was like flying in one of those aircraft.

First, Dick will preface those flying experiences with a short description of an incident that he witnessed while stationed at Griffiss AFB. For those unfamiliar with the design of the C-119 aircraft it looks something like the old WW II P-38 Fighter plane with two engines, one engine mounted in something like a fuselage on each side of the main fuselage, with the wing passing through all three components. The horizontal stabilizer connected the two vertical stabilizers. In the incident at Griffiss AFB the C-119 was on short final when the horizontal stabilizer fell off, leaving the pilot with no ability to control the pitch of the aircraft. Through some very skillful flying, the pilot managed to get the aircraft on the ground in a large enough piece that all personnel on board survived with only minor injuries. That incident was always fresh in Dick's mind whenever he flew on the C-119. Incidentally, during Dick's years in the Air Force, he had many opportunities to fly on the C-119 aircraft.

Travel to Athens was uneventful with a stop in Rome, Italy for refueling. The troops got off the aircraft briefly while refueling to stretch the old legs from the overly uncomfortable seats and then it was off to Athens. There was no time for sightseeing; however they did get to see some of the main features of Rome from the air as they departed.

Finally the four airmen arrived in Athens and they eventually found out their ultimate destination. They were going to Incirlik AFB in Turkey, near the City of Adana. For a detailed description of the activities at Incirlik AFB please read the book, "Operation Overflight" written by Gary Francis Powers. Incidentally, within the next few months Dick would get to know who the U-2 pilots were as a group however, due to the criticality of their mission they did not mingle with others on the base. In fact, their mission was so classified, according to Power's book that when they were flying they did not know where they were going, had no idea where they had been or what they had done. In addition, all outgoing mail from the base was censured, meaning, any reference to the base or its mission was physically removed by razor blade.

Once in Athens, again the four airmen had to wait for a flight into Turkey. They had a total of about three days while waiting for a flight and they made great use of that time. Dick had his brand new camera and took advantage of that time to photograph many of the historic sites in and around Athens. The four guys hired a guide (a very good guide I might add) to insure they visited as many of the sites as possible.

Finally the day arrived when the four guys would eventually reach their final destination; however there were still a few thrills awaiting them. Again they would fly on the old reliable C-119 cargo plane. This air craft was basically a cargo plane designed primarily to carry cargo and not troops; therefore it would be helpful to know a little about the interior layout of the plane when carrying troops. First, all seats known as bucket seats (such as they were) were simply a piece of canvas hanging from the side of the plane, with a seat belt attached to the floor below. Large cargo that was strapped in the center of the plane was generally only two or three feet in front of the troops. When a person was seated in the bucket seat your butt was generally only a few inches above the floor, thus very uncomfortable.

Next there were no latrines (known as rest rooms in civilian parlance) in the craft but not to worry. There was a tube rising out of the floor in the center of the plane with a four to six inch funnel attached that served as a urinal. Any other urges you may have had apparently were left in your pants.

Now that you have some appreciation for the interior design of the aircraft, let the fun begin. It didn't take long for the first adventure. The day was hot, very hot in fact and the plane was overloaded, and thus it took three attempts to get airborne. Each try would burn off some fuel until the plane finally got light enough to fly.

As already stated the day was hot and the air was rough, therefore looking out the back of the plane you could clearly see the tail section of the plane flopping in many directions, bringing back memories of the incident at Griffiss just a few months before. Add to that, the fact that it was absolutely against Air Force Regulations to ditch in a C-119, the only other option was to jump. The reason for no ditching was the fact that the C-119 had the flotation characteristics of a rock.

As the flight wore on the flying became much rougher and more and more troops found it necessary to use the highly "private" toilet facilities. Try to imagine standing in the middle of the plane, attempting to hold the funnel with one hand, while trying to stabilize yourself by holding on to a post in the center of the craft for support. All this time you are attempting to urinate in a small funnel as the plane was bouncing in all directions in very turbulent air with urine going most every place but in the funnel. In fact most of the urine went on your hands, shoes, floor and pants; all this time some fifty to sixty troops cheering your every miss. There was one consolation though; virtually no one could hold it for the duration of the flight, so you would get your chance to cheer for others.

Finally the joy ride was over and they landed at their new home. Keep in mind the year was 1956 and the site was shared by both American and Turkish personnel, with the Americans on one side of the base and the Turks on the other. Basically the Turks were there to protect the base and the Americans were there to support the flying mission, namely the U-2s, the reason for such high security.

It was finally time to meet the new boss, Squadron Commander Captain C. (the most unforgettable character Dick ever met) and the First Sergeant whom Dick will refer to as Tom. Sergeant Tom would give his four new troops the grand tour, get them acquainted with their new barracks (a big change from Griffiss), introduce them to all the other Weather Personnel, and particularly the Weather Station etc.

So what was unique about Incurlik Air Force Base? First, it is located in the middle of the desert some 20 to 40 miles north of the eastern end of the Mediterranean Sea, where it is extremely dry year round with humidity levels generally below 10% throughout the year. Summertime temperatures reached 120 degrees or more nearly every day with nighttime temperatures getting all the way down to maybe 95 degrees.

The barracks were 1900 vintage Quonset huts that were built even before they had been invented. The huts were probably about 20 feet across and approximately 50 feet long. Each hut would hold approximately twenty men in single deck beds and double that number when a second bed was attached above. Heat was supplied in the winter by a kerosene fired space heater in the center of the hut that produced enough heat to warm a ten foot circle. So you may wonder why you would need heat in a place like this. Temperatures in the winter were often down into the 30 to 40 degree range with frequently very strong winds and, the Quonset hut had no insulation or weather stripping to keep the wind out, or the heat in. These buildings were as cold in the winter as they were hot in the summer.

Summer air conditioning; of which there was none, was much better in that you could take nearly all the skin off the hut thus allowing for plenty of air. Sleeping was an oxymoron. Everyone slept as near to the raw as physically possible with the bed soaked in water (sweat) while the exposed skin was bone dry.

Latrine (toilet) facilities were located in a similar building some 75 to 100 feet away that supported three or four barracks. In the summer you could go to the latrine in a pair of shorts, jump in the shower and by the time you got back to the barracks you would be completely dry.

How about entertainment? Well, there were card games most any time during the day. Take your choice; Hearts, Cribbage and Pinnacle were the most common choices, no gambling was allowed. There were also no lights allowed during the night since virtually everyone was working on rotating shifts. During the day and in the summer there were almost always enough guys to get up a game of softball or football. Believe it or not, in that 120 degree heat all sports were almost always played in sweat suits—a trick learned from the Turks.

Your next most logical question would/should be why did you need something to occupy your time? Well, as Dick explained earlier, there was a severe shortage of Weather Observers worldwide; however not in Turkey. In Turkey they had so many Observers they only worked two days out of every six. Why did they have so many, particularly when they averaged only about 20 days a year of IFR (Instrument Flight Rules) weather? That was just another one of those great mysteries of life.

How about movies? There were movies virtually every night as soon as it became dark enough in the large outdoor theater. You see the screen was four pieces of plywood (painted white), affixed to a couple of large poles set in the ground. Seats were plush orange crates (or boxes) that could be moved to any location you chose. The movies were generally good, plus the movie also had the added benefit of wasting a couple of hours of "precious" idle time. Once in a while they got a treat and could watch the movie in the middle of a sand storm, necessitating you to keep your face covered and peeking at the movie between your fingers.

Incidentally, sandstorms were always a lot of fun, especially after they were over, giving you the opportunity to get the sand out of your bed, your clothes, your hair and everything else you owned. The Quonset hut barracks provided virtually no protection against the sandstorm.

Mornings, or more importantly any time you were getting dressed, always gave you a chance for some excitement. You see, any time you got dressed, or were simply changing clothes there was a standard routine. You dumped your shoes, shook out your socks and all the rest of your clothes to insure you did not have a scorpion or centipede hiding therein. Scorpions were smaller but otherwise similar to those found in the southern U.S. (maybe two inches long), whereas the centipedes were four to five inches long, with a hundred legs on each side. Scorpions could only sting, whereas the centipede could both sting and also do great damage with the pinchers in their mouth, thus the getting dressed routine.

Mail Call was always a big event as it generally occurred only once a week; however once in a great while there would be a second Mail Call within a week. With Weather personnel working very closely with Base Operations, they generally were some of the first to know about scheduled incoming aircraft that could be carrying mail, thus news travelled fast. Upon arrival, mail was processed quickly and Mail Call time was posted as soon as possible. It usually took the rest of that day to catch up reading all of the mail.

How about the chow? It was generally fair to good excepting those times when for whatever reason fresh food could not be delivered to the base, which didn't happen too often. When it did happen k-rations got awfully tiresome.

Periodically, the base would schedule a bus to take interested persons on site seeing trips to nearby points of interest on a Sunday. For example, Dick got a chance to visit St Paul's First Church of Antioch as described in the Biblical New Testament on one such trip. The church was physically located in the little town of Tarsus. St Paul was born and lived in Tarsus as a Jew named Saul until after his conversion. After converting he made numerous missionary trips to the Roman Empire and in either AD 64 or AD 67 he was beheaded by Emperor Nero on June 29. After Saint Paul's death Tarsus continued as an important city and became a part of the Byzantine Empire.

The actual church does not look much like a conventional church, but rather more like a large cave built into the side of a rock cliff. The front has some carvings and the interior contains a relatively large carved alter.

It was time to try something different for a change, so one morning during the week a group of the guys decided to take a ride on the train. The train was the old Berlin to Bagdad Express, made famous during the First World War. The train travelled from Berlin, Germany to Bagdad in Turkey. The railroad was actually built during the First World War, thus the cars and equipment were of the same vintage with steam locomotives and comparable cars. The guys plan was to get on the very historic train in Adana and ride it to Mercin down on the coast, then return. The plan was going well until the train suddenly stopped out in the middle of nowhere. Many of the passengers got off, took out their prayer rugs and everyone assumed they all faced Mecca and began daily prayers.

The group of guys was all seated in the very last car on the train when the conductor suddenly made everyone get off the train, out in the middle of nowhere. Everyone collectively thought this was going to be a very long walk back to Adana. Finally the conductor made everyone understand they simply wanted to put them all in a different car. They moved the entire group from the very last car on the train to the very first car behind the locomotive. Apparently everyone had first class tickets and they had been seated in a third class car. The car where they had been seated had wooden seats and was not the cleanest. The car they moved everyone into must have been first class with overstuffed seats and everything was spic and span. The return ride home was in the same car.

Occasionally a group of guys would go into Adana to see the sites. A place you had to see was Ataturk Park. Ataturk is to Turkey the same as George Washington is to the United States. Many Parks and major buildings are named after him, as well as many statues. Another place that provided a unique experience was a walk through the residential area. The sidewalk was simply an extension of the street of about eight to ten feet. The apartment buildings then connected to the side walk. Many of the apartment buildings were three or four stories high with a balcony projecting out over the sidewalk. The balcony appeared to be the favorite bathroom as frequently someone would park their butt on the balcony rail and just let her go, both liquid and solid, so without constant attention to activities above, you could end up with a shower or a plotcher. Essentially the street and sidewalk was one big sewer.

Another favorite spot to visit was the Seyhan River and the great stone bridge that was built by Alexander the Great in antiquity. That bridge was the only way to cross the river and according to the internet it still remains functional yet today; however a new bridge has been built for modern traffic. You were never sure what you might see when crossing this bridge, for example there was a murder in town on New Year's Eve the year Dick was there. The murderer was caught and within three or four days he was hanged from one of the light poles on the bridge, and left there for four or five days as a reminder that crime did not pay in Adana.

The Seyhan River was also the primary water supply for Adana, but it was also the favorite spot to take a bath and wash your horse and buggy.

When travelling off base there was another Turkish custom that took a bit to get your arms around. Toilet facilities were unisex with bomb site toilets. For those unfamiliar, they were quite simply a hole in the floor with treads to place your feet. The object was to hit the hole without getting feet and clothing dirty. Harder still was learning to use their toilet paper, as it was called your hand! In high class places there was a faucet close by for washing your hand. If travelling by bus a pit stop was just that. The bus stopped along the road, everyone got off and you picked your spot. Since you always carried your toilet paper (your left hand) it was never a big deal.

Generally speaking there was not too much exciting going on while in Turkey, but one day, a three or four day adventure materialized out of nowhere. There was another guy involved; however Dick does not remember his name so we will just call him Hank. First Dick must begin this story by stating the fact that we had very little air traffic into this base, even though we had one of the largest runways in Europe. Virtually all flying was done by U-2 aircraft, and even they were rare. The one type of aircraft that did arrive occasionally was our favorite C-119 cargo plane which nearly always brought MAIL, and they rarely arrived more than once or twice a week.

This adventure began with the arrival of a C-119 aircraft. Apparently, there were orders on board to select two long time guys and advise them they had been selected to go to Burton Woods, England to participate in an all Europe softball tournament. How Hank and Dick's names got on the list is another one of those great mysteries of life, since there were no organized softball teams on the base. In any case they had forty-five minutes to get their duds together and be on the plane.

Once on the plane and on their way they got the rest of the story. They were scheduled to stop in Athens, refuel the aircraft and then fly direct to Tripoli, Libya where they would meet other potential players from around Europe. From there another plane would take the whole group to Burton Woods, England for the tournament.

After a fairly long, uneventful ride they arrived in Tripoli where they got the full story. First things first, the plane going to England had serious mechanical difficulties and the whole adventure had been cancelled, thus everyone was on their own to get back from whence you came.

The next big adventure was everyone was required to receive about an hour long briefing before going *ANYPLACE*. This briefing described the customs of the country and how you interact with the natives. For a young eighteen year old kid, fresh off the farm, this was a quite an eye opener. Dick doesn't remember much of the briefing except that part about driving a vehicle. If you were driving a vehicle, of any kind, and you were unfortunate enough to hit a native, there were certain steps that must be taken immediately. The *VERY FIRST STEP YOU MUST TAKE WAS TO BACK UP AND RUNOVER THEM AGAIN,* several times in fact. In fact you would run over them as many times as it took to be absolutely certain they were dead. Why you might ask. If the victim was dead there was no penalty, however; if the victim was alive, you the driver must take care of them for the rest of their lives. That advice was for openers, however; there was much more, but unimportant for this story.

In any case Hank and Dick's main objective at this point was to leave, going any place east that would get them back to Turkey, such as Rome or Athens. To succeed with this plan, they would need to spend much time in Base Operations where they could check every aircraft arrival and planned departure. On the third day the inbound board showed a C-119 aircraft bound for Athens. That was just the flight they were looking for. When the pilot (a very young Lieutenant) came into operations, the guys approached him to see if he would take them with him to Athens. His reply was that he didn't have enough flight time to carry passengers: however there was possibly an alternative. He said if they had Currier Orders he would be obligated to take them along. Dick and Hank told him that their headquarters were across the street and they would see him soon.

Upon arriving at headquarters, they identified their predicament and requested any assistance. Headquarters gave them the needed Currier Orders, plus something to carry. Each guy got a unique light bulb, only used on Weather Equipment to carry back to Incurlik AFB, thus qualifying them for the Orders.

Back at Base Operations they located their Lieutenant, presented him with a copy of their orders, and they were then on their way back to Athens. Once in Athens, the travelers discovered something new about being Curriers, that is, once you are identified as a Currier, everyone in the world knows, and you are assisted in every way possible to get you to your destination, as quickly as possible. That said, the next morning, bright and early, a C-119 was scheduled to fly to Incurlik AFB and Hank and Dick were on it. All in all, Hank and Dick were gone from Turkey for nearly a week to play softball, but never once got "up to bat". This trip to Libya however did convince Dick of one thing. If he was ever to get another chance to return to Libya, don't. Of all the places he has been, that is the only one he has no desire to return to.

Dick had now been in Turkey, or at least out of the country for over one year, thus it was now getting time to seriously begin to think about returning stateside.

Orders arrived in early October indicating Dick would be reassigned to Homestead Air Force Base located on the very southern tip of Florida. The reporting date for his new assignment would be on or about December 1, 1958; therefore he would be returning stateside in early November.

One of the final tasks just prior to leaving Turkey was to wish all of his many new lifelong friends a fond farewell.

Joy Ann Blood, his fiancée, could now complete final plans for the anticipated wedding, purchase a car, and gather all of her personal belongings that would be needed to go to Florida, etc.

The wedding would be very small, with only families and a few close friends in attendance. After getting away for a couple of days following the wedding it was time to pack the car and soon begin the long trip south to Florida.

The car that Joy Ann had purchased, with the help of her father, was a 1954 nine passenger Ford Station Wagon which was perfect for the task at hand. They would load virtually all their belongings into the car for the trip south. Dick had almost nothing but a very few clothes and his uniforms since he had been in the military virtually all of his adult life. Joy Ann had some dishes, pots and pans, enough food to get started and other necessities that they would need to set up an apartment and the car was full.

They had to be at Homestead AFB by the first of December; however there was much that had to get done. Incidentally Joy Ann did not have her driver's license yet at that time so Dick had to do all the driving. Once reaching Homestead, there was much to be done, things neither Joy Ann nor Dick had had any experience with. The first big item to get accomplished was to locate an apartment and get settled into that, and with help from the base that was not a large task; however with military pay you couldn't afford much. Basically they found a two room apartment, with NO heat and NO air conditioning. The apartment complex was in one long building similar to a motel with seven two room apartments in the building. The apartments in this complex were generally all occupied by military personnel.

It was now time to get back to work. Homestead AFB was much different than any of the others where Dick had been stationed in that it had a much larger Weather Station and many more aircraft assigned to the base. At that time there were two Wings of B-47 bombers and a Squadron of KC-97 refueling aircraft for a total of some one hundred to one hundred fifty aircraft. With that many aircraft there was much more activity in the Weather Station.

Dick's job in this environment was also much different than before. With many more personnel in the group, his seniority ran out and he returned to shift work with rotating shifts. Essentially that meant working two midnight shifts, two day shifts and two swing shifts, then two days off.

There was a big plus though in going back on shift work. With all of the flying, much of which was during the day, the day shift was generally very busy; however the second and third shifts were generally less hectic unless there was a mission in progress. With more time available, Dick was generally able to spend significant amounts of time working with the forecasters. It was not long before they allowed him to begin analyzing the various charts that he had just plotted, time permitting.

As Dick gained more and more experience, the forecasters' began allowing him to work with them on actually preparing pilot briefings, then even allowing him to participate in the briefings. This was a great time for Dick since he had always been interested in the weather for as long as he could remember.

By gaining all of this "hands on" experience, Dick was leaning more and more towards remaining in the Air Force and then attending Weather Forecasting school, but as you will see that was not part of the grand plan, as *DESTINY* would have it's say.

With all the additional aircraft and much more bad weather ever present there was also a requirement to have a Weather Observer stationed right on the approach end of the active runway whenever IFR (bad weather) was forecast, which was much of the time. Being out there was quite a thrill, for you see there was a small shack situated right on the end of the runway where you were stationed. On final approach the large aircraft generally would pass right above your shack within 50 to 100 feet, or close enough to check the air in their tires.

One day when Dick was on his way out to the runway shack he had a very unusual event occur. The base motor pool provided the vehicle and driver to get you out to your runway position and in order to get there you needed to wind your way through all those aircraft. Suddenly, there were frogs wherever you looked; on the ground, on the aircraft, and on the vehicle, essentially everywhere, by the thousands. Dick had read about this phenomenon, but that was the only time he had ever seen it. This unusual phenomenon is caused when a tornado, or more likely a waterspout touches down and sucks those little critters up into the cloud then drops them some distance away. The phenomenon has also been observed with fish.

Excitement was rare in Florida but there was one event that may be worth mentioning. The story actually began nearly four years earlier while Dick was in Basic Training at Sampson AFB. The various events were usually scheduled several days in advance, apparently to give you a chance to get prepared. This particular event was to learn how to jump into a deep (10 feet or more) pool with nothing but a barracks bag as a flotation device. Let me begin by stating Dick had never been in water deeper than his knees except when swimming in the Mediterranean where it was impossible to sink with your head under water. During Basic Training it was clearly stated that you would either jump willingly or you would be thrown in. Dick was petrified while waiting for that day to arrive. The fateful day finally arrived and when Dick checked the duty roster for that day he discovered he was scheduled for guard duty all that day, thus he missed all the fun.

Now back to Florida. One of the guys and his wife that Dick worked with lived in a trailer park that had a swimming pool and they invited Dick and Joy over to take a dip in the their pool. The weather was exceedingly hot and Dick and Joy had no air conditioning in their apartment so they thought that was a great idea.

It is now time to set the stage for the great adventure. Remember Dick had never, ever been in a swimming pool or even in water above his knees except as stated above. He did not know that just because the water was only three feet deep where he was standing that it could be totally different someplace else within the pool. Thus he had been dog paddling around in the three foot deep water when he suddenly decided to swim to the other end of the pool.

At about half way across he was beginning to get tired so he decided to stand up for a rest. SURPRISE, SURPRISE! Now he is standing on the bottom of the pool with no idea how to get back to the surface. After giving the situation a few seconds thought he knew that if he started walking back in the direction from whence he came, the water would be much shallower, and thus it was so. After walking back a few steps he came to the ledge and suddenly breathing became much better. He had just learned life lesson number 35 (learn how to swim early in life; you never know when you may need it).

There was generally not a lot to do while in Florida, or more importantly, there was not much money to do it with, however Dick and Joy were able to take a few day trips into the southern Florida area. Joy Ann had heard about Sanibel Island on the west coast of Florida where collecting sea shells was supposedly at its very best, therefore they decided to take a drive over there on one of Dick's days off. They did indeed find a great variety of shells that made the trip well worth their time.

Another day trip that they took was a drive down to Key West. If you have a fear of bridges, this is not the trip for you to take. Also a trip through the Everglades is interesting however there is not a lot of variety, but many alligators (if that is your thing).

Occasionally following a heavy rain, one of the guys Dick worked with had a small caliber rifle that he and Dick would use to go out into the everglades and shoot the big rattle snakes that had been driven out of the canals; otherwise, there was not much excitement while stationed in Florida.

With about three or four months left to go on his enlistment it was beginning to be time to start considering his future. He had received his fourth stripe making him a Staff Sargent which just complicated his decision. There were several other factors that needed to be considered. First, there was a massive reduction in the military and a two months early discharge was very common. Second, Joy Ann had been extremely homesick the entire time they were in Florida and she did not like the military life style. Third, with the cutbacks taking place in the military the possibility of advancing into the forecasting field had now become very problematic.

Events happened rapidly starting about mid-July when Dick received new orders that his discharge date had been moved from October 14th to August 14th or his enlistment had been reduced by sixty days. Apparently there was no longer a decision to be made as the Air Force had removed any option of remaining in the military. Dick and Joy had already decided that they would return north and settle in the village of Remsen, NY where Joy had grown up. There were numerous reasons for that decision such as; reasonable housing, more opportunities for employment, family, etc.

Joy's father was a Town Supervisor in the Town of Remsen, NY and he had arranged for Dick to get a job working for the County of Oneida in upgrading an old TB Hospital into a Home for The Aged in the City of Utica. It resulted in a significant reduction in pay from the Air Force, but he had to begin somewhere considering he had all the skills of someone just getting out of high school.

There was one good side to this job. Dick would be working with two or three excellent craftsmen and he would have the opportunity to learn many skills that would serve him well throughout his lifetime. He learned about electrical wiring, plumbing and carpentry plus other areas too numerous to mention.

Looking back over the past sixty years Dick believes he made the correct decision based on the situation at that time. Here are the hard cold facts; Dick was nearly 21 years old with virtually no education and no marketable skills when he went into the work force. NOTE: That is the situation that nearly every young person faced then, as they do now when they choose their country first.

In the 1950's there was a mandatory draft where everyone was required to serve for two years in the military unless they could get an exemption from serving. There were a few qualifying reasons to get an exemption. The most common were: (1) Farm exemption (not extensively used since it required too much hard work), (2) College Exemption (extensively used – not too expensive then, provided a good time, many individuals got multiple degrees to continue the exemption throughout their entire draft eligibility years) or (3) Get married and become a father (used extensively). NOTE: The college exemption proved extremely beneficial for many young men for a couple of reasons: 1) it allowed them to avoid serving in the military in any capacity and 2) it generally added at least four more years to their company benefits such as vacation and retirement.

Many of Dick's generation used Option 2 above to evade military service, went to school, had a good time, got a good job and had the option to spend 30-40 years with a company that provided them with a great pension. Well guess what. That is all they have ever done, having never done one damn thing in their entire life except make money so that in old age all they can do is go to the bank and count it, then worry about how they are going to liquidate their assets. Very few people have found a way to take it with them, and if they have they are not letting anyone else in on the secret.

For Dick, he has done things that the vast majority of people cannot even dream of, thus he has the memories and the stories to go with them. Also don't forget there comes a time in everyone's life when all you have left is memories. That too Dick knows. So once again Dick and Joy packed their few belongings into the old Ford Wagon and headed north.

Once they got settled into their new environment Dick realized the only real education that he had was the Air Force Tech School (Air Weather School) while in the Air Force. He also discovered he had the reading capability of about a Fifth Grader, therefore he decided it was time to change all of that. So what to do? He started buying books, many books and started to study them. Each night after supper he would take those books to bed, along with his trusty dictionary and he LEARNED to read and comprehend those many books. It worked. However, the greatest lesson he learned, contrary to popular opinion, NO ONE can force you to learn anything. The greatest minds in the world are almost universally SELF EDUCATED. Life is not about studying for the NEXT TEST as in school, but rather studying for that next great adventure that is just waiting around the corner, waiting to be discovered. Dick hopes you will enjoy the many adventures that he has had the opportunity to be a part of, for there are many, many more waiting for you to read about.

Chapter Three

THE TRANSITIONAL YEARS

Life was about to become very different than anything Dick had previously experienced. Four years earlier, Dick had lived his entire life at home on the family farm, followed by four more years in the military. In each case food and shelter had always been provided. That scenario was about to change dramatically. After Dick and Joy were married and had moved to Florida they were no longer dependent on their families or the military for food and lodging as had been the case throughout their lives previously. At that time the military was much more like a job than simply a different way of life.

They had to provide their own shelter (apartment) and food instead of simply going to the military chow hall for each and every meal. They had to pay rent for their apartment and had to go to the grocery store after planning their meals to purchase the food. However these tasks and life changes were not unique to Dick and Joy as every young couple faces the same challenges.

There was another major change for Dick in particular since he had never had a job, so to speak, throughout his entire life. As previously stated Dick had worked hard all of his entire life, however he had never received pay for his work, therefore he had never managed money, in fact he had never had any money to manage. This aspect of his life was completely new and was a skill that he would need to develop and perfect very quickly.

The first order of business after returning to Remsen was to locate a place to live that they could afford. Joy's family was a great help in assisting them in locating a two family house with an apartment that they could rent out that would significantly assist them in paying the mortgage, taxes and other expenses. Again Dick's relatively new father-in-law, being a local county politician had political connections and negotiated a position for him with Oneida County in working on the upgrading of an old TB Hospital into a home for the infirm. This job although very low paying, allowed him to acquire numerous skills that would be very useful throughout his life. For example he worked with three very skilled craftsmen, one a carpenter, one an electrician and one a plumber. In addition they were rebuilding the on-site resident home of the facility Director. That portion of the facility that provided Dick with the most experience was the complete rebuilding and remodeling of the large kitchen.

Dick worked for the County for about one year when he received an opportunity to get a job that paid substantially more money. As with most political jobs, this one had required each employee to pay tribute to the controlling political party which was very difficult for Dick to accept.

The new job was working for a Heavy Equipment Company (no longer in business) as a Sales Clerk and a "Go-For", not a very impressive job title, but as you will see it changed Dick's life completely. Not long after starting there, management discovered Dick had numerous skills that they could use in preparing a new building for a shop and office. This building was located some distance east of Utica with remodeling taking place during the coldest part of winter by the Manager and Dick.

Since the weather was very cold and there was no heat in the building that was being renovated, Dick and his boss would eat their lunch in a heated building that was used part time as an office.

"DESTINY" was about to reappear. While setting in this building, just passing time, Dick was looking for something to read, anything in fact. What he found was an old telephone directory, complete with some yellow pages.

While thumbing through those pages he discovered an advertisement for the Utica School of Commerce. They were advertising a new course that would teach you how to wire and operate EAM (Electronic Accounting Machines). Since before joining the Military Dick had been interested in attending an electronics trade school, but due to inadequate funds he decided to join the Air Force instead; therefore, just maybe this could be something he would be interested in.

After calling the school, they convinced him he should stop over and look around. Dick and Joy accepted the offer to visit the Utica School of Commerce the next evening.

This was Dick's first introduction to IBM Cards (EAM) as he had never even heard of a punched card. For anyone unfamiliar with those cards they were approximately 3 inches high by about seven inches long with each card containing 80 columns across and 12 rows top to bottom. Each column could contain one alpha-numeric character; therefore each card could contain eighty alpha-numeric characters.

The cost for the course was $150 for one week or five classes. The next night Dick and Joy discussed that information with Joy's parents and they were convinced it was a total scam and a complete waste of money. You may think $150 should not be much of a decision, but back in those days that was more than a month's rent. They went ahead and spent the money and as you will see it was probably the best money Dick ever spent since virtually everything throughout the rest of his life was a direct result of spending those one hundred fifty dollars.

A short time after attending the Utica School of Commerce, the job at the Heavy Equipment Dealer was completed and Dick received his Layoff Notice. Once again he got a political job with the Oneida County Highway Department as a heavy equipment operator for the summer.

As soon as Dick finished the Wiring course at the Utica School of Commerce he immediately began visiting all of the Businesses in the Utica/Rome area where he thought they may be using IBM equipment and submitted an application for employment. Things were not looking good as there was virtually no interest for anyone recently out of the service and someone, with no experience and no degree. However he was confident there was someone out there, some place that would give him a chance.

Each night when Dick got home from work he checked the Utica newspaper for advertisements for someone, anyone, looking for an EAM (Electronic Accounting Machine) Operator. It was on a Wednesday night towards the end of summer when there was an advertisement for just such a job with RCA Service Company, located at Griffiss Air Force Base. The job was for the night shift and it gave a contact name. The minimum requirements for the job was a college degree AND two years' experience, unfortunately (Dick was a little short, NO a lot short on all counts).

Little did Dick know that today would be the day *"DESTINY"* would reappear again after a long absence.

The first thing Thursday morning Dick gave RCA a call and the conversation went something like so:

Dick: Good morning, this is Mahlon Palmer and I am calling in regards to your advertisement in last nights' newspaper that indicates you are seeking an EAM Operator, and that all inquiries should be directed to the Point of Contact whom we will call Jack.

Jack: Can you tell me a little about yourself.

Dick: I am currently employed by the Oneida County Highway Department as a Heavy Equipment Operator; however I recently completed a course at Utica School of Commerce where I learned to wire EAM equipment such as IBM 514 Reproducing Punch, IBM 557 Card interpreter and 087 Collator. I also recently received my Honorable Discharge from the Air Force after serving four years where I attained the rank of Staff Sargent with a career in the Air Weather Service. Incidentally, attaining the rank of Staff Sergeant in a four year enlistment in the Air Force is not unheard of however, it is also not common, and in regard to your last requirement I have no college education.

Jack: Well you don't have anything that we can use at this time, however if you would care to come in on Saturday we would be happy to talk to you and you could fill out an application at that time.

Dick: I was in a while ago and completed an application then, however I will be out of town this weekend so maybe I could come in sometime next week.

Jack: Well, are you busy this afternoon? If not, could you come in today?

Dick: I can meet with you this afternoon, see you soon.

Dick immediately took the afternoon as vacation, went home, got out his best clothes (nothing fancy just clean new slacks, white shirt and tie with a sport coat) and headed for Griffiss AFB.

Dick met with Jack and the line of questioning followed a similar line as the phone conversation, except there was much more detail, particularly regarding his military service and experiences. They had no other ex-military employees and certainly no one else with Dick's experiences.

The next question was "How much would you need to come to work?"

Dick's response was he would need at least $75.00 per week. At this point Jack excused himself and left the room for a few minutes.

When he came back he said he was sorry but they could not pay $75.00 a week (Things had gone so well Dick was genuinely disappointed) then Jack finished the sentence. We don't pay that low, if you want the job you will need to take $85.00 dollars a week, plus 10% night shift bonus, since we are offering you a job on the night shift. Dick thought he had fallen into Hog Heaven as this was the greatest news he had had since leaving the Air Force.

Friday morning Dick went to work at the Oneida County Highway Department and thanked them for giving him the opportunity to work there while looking for more permanent employment and then he submitted his two week notice to terminate his employment.

Along with working, Dick really needed to purchase some new clothes since RCA required, (as we would have said in the Air Force, you must wear a class 'A' uniform) a suit and tie or dress slacks, dress shirt and jacket while at work. Dick totally agreed with that philosophy then as he does today, as the old saying still applies, "*YOU NEVER GET A SECOND CHANCE TO MAKE ANOTHER FIRST IMPRESSION*". To take that philosophy a step further, it has been his experience if you come to work looking like a bum, your work will generally follow that same pattern.

Monday night finally came and Dick was off to his first day of work with RCA where he would meet his new boss, the Second Shift Supervisor whom we will call Joe. There was so much to learn; so where to start. Dick has previously described what an IBM (EAM) card was like for those who are less than thirty years old; remember we are talking about 1958/59.

The first task was to learn how to handle all of those EAM (Electronic Accounting Machine) cards, of which there were thousands, no actually tens of thousands. The prime requirement was to always keep them all in sequence without dropping a tray or even a small hand full. Getting just a few cards out of sequence was almost always as bad as getting a few thousand mixed up thus the requirement to always use great care whenever handling those cards. Learning how to properly handle cards was more difficult and critical than actually running the equipment.

After proper card handling had been perfected it was now time to begin operating the various pieces of equipment. The 083 Card Sorter was where they would start and was used to place a deck (stack, handful or tray full) of cards into sequence based on data that was punched into specified card columns. By the end of the first week he was quite familiar with the 083 Sorter, 087 Collator, 514 Reproducing Punch, 557 Card Interpreter and the 407 Printer/ Calculator. He also had an opportunity to use some of the skills that he had learned at the Utica School of Commerce although he never wired the 407 Calculator/Printer since RCA had one guy that was in charge of that. As you will soon see that was totally unimportant.

By the second week Dick was now ready to focus his full attention on the procedures since each task had detailed step-by-step instructions to insure complete, accurate and consistent results.

It is probably now appropriate to give you a look at the structure of the entire EDP (Electronic Data Processing) organization as it was, as recently as ten years ago.

Manager

Systems Development

Key Punching

EAM Operations-including operating the Computer

The Manager has overall responsibility of the operation, including staffing, payroll, scheduling etc.

Systems Development is by far the most critical task in the entire operation (in my humble opinion). This person or persons must have a very broad range of knowledge, must have outstanding communication skills and extensive management skills. This person(s) must also be able to communicate with upper management as well as entry level personnel and the more knowledge they have relating to the user community the more effective they will be. Staff will generally be Systems Analysts and/or Programmer analysts. More recent terminology would be Systems Architects and Computer Programmers as they compare more favorability with structural architects in the building trades.

Systems Architects interface directly with the user community and are directly responsible for identifying and defining the user requirements. Once the requirements have been defined and approved by the user, the System Architect must design a computer program/process that will produce all of the agreed to reports, inquiries and any other output products. *THEN* the Architect must prepare detailed instructions that will define in great detail the precise products that will be built by the Programmer (builder). The relationship between the Systems Architect and the Programmer is virtually the same as the relationship between a structural Architect and the building contractor.

Key punching is not nearly as critical today as it was just a few years ago due to major advances in technology; therefore you will need to use your imagination. Once again technology has advanced so far and so fast that Dick is not able to comment on it.

Due to major advances in technology, the old requirements to have specialists operate punched card equipment are virtually non-existent. Functions that were critically important as recently as ten years ago may be totally nonexistent in today's world.

By the third week Dick had pretty much mastered all the normal everyday activities, but there was still that IBM 650 *COMPUTER* sitting in the corner that was begging for his attention. The one person who knew all things that Dick wanted to know was the Programmer who worked during the day, so he was not available, therefore Dick needed another plan. Dick had already established a good working relationship with the IBM computer Technician that maintained their hardware so Dick asked if he could get any brochures, training manuals or any other information that he could learn about the computer. In a few days he brought Dick more information than most everyone else had ever seen.

As soon as Dick got the information he began studying during any spare time he had. This was a God send for your typical self-educated person, proving once again you can learn more directly from the horse's mouth than you can from most of your associates. This package contained information about all the working parts inside the machine that most people never take the time to learn; however information that allows you to take full advantage of all the functionality that is not readily apparent.

As a team on the night shift they had a task that was very labor intensive and generally took two people a full shift to complete the work. After having some time to study the new IBM 650 information that Dick had just received, it appeared to him that this particular task could possibly be converted to the computer, thus Dick sat down with the Computer Programmer to discuss the possibility of the programmer developing such a program. He assured Dick they had already investigated that possibility and had determined the task was beyond the capability of their computer so the issue was dropped;

however this became a compelling force for Dick to figure out how it could be accomplished.

Dick was now in his fourth month with RCA and there were staffing changes being made. First the Day Shift Supervisor, Jack was promoted from the First Shift Machine Room Supervisor to a Staff position reporting directly to the newly appointed Computer Center Manager. Then Joe who had been the Second Shift supervisor was promoted to the Day Shift Supervisor position which was now vacant. This second shift position was then offered to Dick even though he had no college degree and only four months of experience; however his four years in the military overcame his lack of formal education with strong management experience and discipline. This new position provided Dick with many new opportunities as you will soon see.

The new position gave him more opportunity and flexibility to pursue his goal of learning all about the IBM 650 computer and developing the program that *could not* be done. Within a month he had an operating proto-type of the program and within another week they had it running in a full blown parallel cycle. Management had great difficulty in accepting the fact that it worked since it had been deemed impossible to build. After a week of failure proof testing it was accepted and reduced their workload by nearly two man days per day.

Another item in the IBM package that was provided by the IBM Technician was a plastic templet used for Flow Charting. Also included was a user's manual that described the purpose of flowcharting, meaning of the symbols and other documentation techniques. For someone who was a self-taught fanatic this was a great start. Building a system or computer program without a flow chart is like building a house without an architect, you never know what you left out until it is finished and you then must go back to rebuild and repair.

From the very beginning Flow Charting became one of the most used tools in Dick's toolbox. Let me try to explain another significant feature. In the development of any computer program or function there is a two-step process involved. The first step is defining, in detail, what you are going to build and the second step is to build what you have planned. In virtually all of Dick's travels educated people combine these two processes into one, under the miss guided assumption you are wasting your time when in reality you generally double your development time. How so, you might ask. When you separate the two activities you can focus your total attention on one activity or the other *WITHOUT* flip-flopping back and forth between design and construction. That's *ENOUGH* about technique.

After just a few successes with writing programs, many more opportunities began coming Dick's way which just presented more great opportunities to learn.

Word travelled fast about Dick's programming activities and by the time he had been with RCA for only six months he had the opportunity to meet the Assistant to the Project Manager, whom we will call Mr. Roberts who reported directly to the Project Manager, both of whom would have major impacts on Dick's career for the next dozen years.

Dick's programming career up to now, (all five or six months) had been on the IBM 650 computer. This computer, being one of the very first business computers was considered a FIRST Generation computer, meaning its logic electronics operated using vacuum tube technology, vacuum tubes like those used in older generation radios. The programming language was SOAP II (Symbolic Optimum Assembly Program—Second Edition). This programming language was just slightly better than machine language.

There was beginning to be rumors about replacing the IBM 650 computer with the much newer IBM 1401, the new Second Generation computer meaning the electronics had been upgraded to transistor technology. There were significant benefits in using the newer technology due to higher speed, much greater reliability, much lower power consumption and much lower heat output to name a few. After hearing these rumors Dick's immediate reaction was to somehow, some way find a way to learn this new programming language so he would be ready as soon as the opportunity presented itself. The avenue he chose was to go back to IBM and obtain a correspondence course that was designed specifically for that purpose. Interestingly, none of the educated crowd thought of pursuing new training; however, as you will soon see the payoffs were huge.

Now it is time to tell you a little about RCA. At this time RCA was a large company that was comprised of several smaller companies such as: Random House Books, Cornet Industries, Hertz Rent-Car, and RCA Service Company to name a few. The one we are going to be primarily interested in will be RCA Service Company that had responsibility for all Government Contracts-World Wide.

In the late 1950's RCA was awarded a very large contract to build and operate the Ballistic Missile Early Warning System (BMEWS) that was designed to locate and track any objects, such as missiles that were approaching the United States from Russia over the North

Pole. There were initially three sites: one located at Thule Greenland, one located at Clear Alaska and a third located at Burton Wood, England. BMEWS was designed to supplement/augment the DEW Line which had previously been built to detect any low flying aircraft that was approaching Canada and the U.S. from Russia. This line of RADAR sites stretched from the very western coast of Alaska, along the northern coast line of Canada, across central Greenland and then down to Iceland. A few years later in Dick's career with RCA he would spend a great deal of time at those sites.

With all the interest in obtaining a second generation IBM computer, RCA had recently entered the Computer field with their own THIRD generation computer, the Spectra 70 Series. The third generation series took computer development to the next level namely going from transistor technology to integrated circuit technology. This time the upgrade took place and they installed the RCA Spectra 70-15 computer system. Fortunately for Dick, his time spent in learning the IBM 1400 Series programming language was very applicable with the only major difference being the Spectra 70 software was significantly more powerful. In addition, RCA would be converting from a completely card based system to essentially a magnetic tape based system. Incidentally not only did they install a third generation computer *BUT IT WAS THE FIRST THIRD GENERATION COMPUTER INSTALLED IN ANY U.S. GOVERNMENT INSTALLTION.*

So guess what, since Dick was the only one who had prepared for this eventuality, he became the Lead Programmer on the project. Again his military training and experience played a key role in this significant promotion. In his new role Dick would first need to develop callable (meaning they could be used in multiple different applications) subroutines that could be used by anyone that needed to access the new tape files.

There would be many programs required that would prepare the numerous reports that had previously been prepared using the IBM 407 printers, therefore several of the EAM Operators would be trained to write those programs using a software package called RPG (Report Program Generator), however this software package could not be used for any serious data manipulation or calculations.

With the installation of the Spectra 70-15 computer complete and the conversion of all those thousands of IBM cards to magnetic tape it was now time for Dick to move on to his next adventure.

Previously Dick has spoken about Mr. Roberts and his boss the BMEWS Project Manager whom we will refer to as Mr. Vincent, both of whom had been transferred to Contract Headquarters in Riverton, New Jersey. They would become the core part of a specialized team of individuals who coordinated all aspects of new business proposals within RCA Service Company. This will be the first time you will hear about Dick's involvement with that team, but it will certainly not be the last.

Within a few days after wrapping up the installation of the Spectra 70-15 computer installation at Griffiss AFB, Dick received a phone call from Mr. Roberts, who had just recently received a promotion to Group Leader of New Business Proposals. This time RCA had received a major enhancement to a Navy contract located on Andros Island in the Bahamas with the acronym of AUTEC (Atlantic Underwater Test and Evaluation Center) and he wanted to know if Dick would be interested in working with him on that contract. Before even knowing what the task was Dick told him he could do it because he wanted to go to the Bahamas.

In all seriousness the task was to build a logistics system for that contract. Actually, Dick had never built a logistics computer system, or any other type of computer system for that matter before, so prior to even getting started he had three strikes against him. Second the computer was a CDC (Control Data Corporation) 3400 of which only three had ever been built and they were located in the University of Montreal, the University of New Mexico and the one at AUTEC. Lastly, the programming language was going to be COBOL, another new programming language that Dick had never used, or even heard of. At Dick's request Mr. Roberts was able to obtain the appropriate computer and programming manuals from CDC so he could get started. Due to the short time frame and critical nature of the assignment, Mr. Roberts was also able to arrange a 3-4 day visit for Dick at CDC Headquarters in Falls Church, Virginia just south of Washington, DC for familiarization and training in the use of COBOL.

Since Dick had absolutely NO systems development experience or training, it was now time to fall back on the old techniques that had served him so well numerous times in the past. You just go back to the old methods used on the farm—when something is broken you must figure out a new way of fixing it and then get on with the day.

As a result of that philosophy, this is the place where the groundwork began to be laid in developing a systems design methodology that Dick would use throughout his entire career. As a side note it was the beginnings of the basic design methodology that Dick would eventually use in designing the largest Inventory Control

System within NASA. That operation was located in Baltimore, Maryland; and controlled all aspects of their warehousing operation that supported literally hundreds of tracking stations around the world. A few years later, this same design methodology would be used by Dick to design and build the largest Accounting System in Lockheed Martin Corporation while working in Utica, New York, on a system that was affectionately known as CORT (Customer Order Requisition Tracking).

With Mr. Roberts being the resident Logistics expert on the new proposal team, Dick and Mr. Roberts were able to put together a very comprehensive and detailed system requirements package. With that information in hand Dick would convert all of that data into his FIRST Computer Systems design package to include: Reports, input/output products, program specifications, file layouts, logic charts, etc.

With Mr. Robert's final approval of the new Logistics system requirements, Dick was now in a position to convert those requirements into detailed program specifications. One could reasonably ask how Dick could prepare program and system specifications if he had never even seen such information before. That would be a very reasonable question. Was it an epiphany, was it Devine Intervention, or, was it just plain "DESTINY"? I guess it will forever just remain one of those great mysteries of life, as we will never know.

The next two to three months were dedicated to converting his newly defined requirements and program specifications into COBOL code. Remember, at this time Dick had no capability to even compile a program (convert code to an actual program) which would allow him to at least identify and correct coding errors.

Finally Dick had completed all that was possible without access to a computer; therefore it was time for him to pack his bags and head south to Andros Island in the Bahamas. He boarded his plane in Syracuse, NY in early April in a heavy snow storm, bound for Miami. From Miami he caught a plane for Andros Island, home of AUTEC.

Welcome to Andros Island, a place where when he stepped off the plane the temperature was in the low 90's and the humidity was over 90%.

Essentially, when you got off the plane on Andros Island you saw the runway, and off in the distance you could see a hotel and a handful of houses. AUTEC employees lived at the hotel and travelled by bus to the site each day.

Incidentally Dick would spend nearly six weeks at Andros before returning home.

Numerous times new employees for AUTEC would arrive on the plane, get off, take a look around, get right back on the same plane and go back to whence they came. There was virtually nothing there.

Once at the site Dick got his first look at a real CDC 3400 computer (remember there were only three of them ever built and he was looking at one of them). This computer was the scientific version of the more popular CDC 3600 business computer (I believe). The primary software used on the 3400 was FORTRAN, designed primarily for scientific applications therefore; the COBOL applications were not really native to this equipment.

Now that Dick had access to THE computer there was much to do. All of those programs must be compiled for the first time, the process that identifies all errors, both coding, spelling and logic. The number of programs has been lost to history but there were many. Finally they were ready to begin serious system testing. Testing on average went very well; however they did identify a few logic errors that would need expert counseling from the Logistics expert, Mr. Roberts when Dick returned to the states.

Time passed quickly and Dick would soon be heading home. Once home he worked closely with the Logistics Expert, Mr. Roberts, where they resolved any and all problems. Dick made necessary program/system modifications and after about a month Dick was ready to head back to Andros.

This time Dick remained on the Island for about two weeks. Time was spent making last minute updates to the system and training all personnel in the use of the new system. Due to the remoteness of the site Dick needed to make sure everyone was up to speed.

Dick will now tell you a little about Andros Island. Andros is the largest island in the Bahamas and is situated along a very deep trench in the ocean named Tongue of The Ocean. This trench is ideally suited for the mission of AUTEC (Atlantic Underwater Test and Evaluation Center). In essence it was designed to test anything that moved through the water or above the water whether it was rockets, missiles, torpedoes, etc. Objects being tested were tracked by radar (above water) and hydrophones (within the water).

Dick had an opportunity to fly down range a couple of times. There was not much to see of the site; however the one thing that struck him the most was the abject poverty those natives lived in.

During Dick's visits to Andros Island, RCA frequently provided minimal entertainment for the employees that worked on the project each Sunday, with a frequent form of entertainment being deep sea fishing. Using one of the boats that was used for chasing torpedoes they would go out quite some distance from the project and then all on board would begin fishing. Just about every type of fish was caught, including several large sharks. Virtually all fish that were caught were taken back and given to the natives for food. Dick went out on several of these trips but was normally quite unsuccessful. However on his last trip out he caught the largest porpoise that they had seen. That fish was also taken back to the natives, right after getting one good souvenir photo.

Vacationing on Andros Island was now over.

On the Monday morning following Dick's return to work from Andros he found a letter lying on his desk. The letter was from Mr. Vincent, the BMEWS Project Manager, Mr. Robert's boss and it was offering him a new job in Riverton, NJ as the only computer specialist on the newly established Proposal Team. Essentially, any time the company was considering bidding on any contract that required computer hardware/software Dick would be assigned. Dick will explain the workings of that team in more detail a little later. The exercise with the *AUTEC* project had far reaching implications over the next several years.

As Dick has mentioned previously that since getting involved with computers and data processing, he believed there were much better ways of designing and implementing systems than what is generally taught in the schools of higher learning. *AUTEC* provided the ideal proving ground for his theories for you see they had complete control of both sides of the equation. Mr. Roberts was the user and Dick was the computer side of the project. Basically, the theories were sound; however they needed to make a few small adjustments in their implementation. Essentially Dick used those techniques and principals throughout his entire career, making a few minor enhancements along the way.

Dick's career spanned nearly thirty years, developing many large computer systems, in many different fields, proving conclusively that individuals charged with building those systems had no requirement to understand those activities in any great detail as Dick will prove a little later in this story. What systems developers MUST have is the ability to listen to the ultimate user/requester's requirements, comprehend and convert what they heard into a detailed plan, and finally obtain the absolute approval from the customer before building can begin.

Building computer systems is very much like building a house. If you have any understanding of building houses the first step (after purchasing the land) is to obtain the services of a competent architect, someone who will listen to your needs/requirements, etcetera, consider laws and restrictions and ultimately provide you with a detailed plan for your approval. Once you are satisfied with the plan you will hire a contractor to build your house. May be, just maybe that is why people who design computer systems in today's world are called systems architects, who then work with the programmers who build and implement the system from detailed system specifications. Dick's experience has been, if you want repeated successes time after time, the above formulae will work *every time*, in any size business or on any project as Dick has worked in them all.

Dick's new assignment in Riverton, NJ was with a small team of about fifteen individuals, each with a unique talent, such as; computers (Dick's), finance, engineering, accounting, personnel, logistics (Mr. Robert's) etcetera. Essentially this was a part time job as they all had a regular job also; Dick being a systems analyst (Systems Architect in today's parlance) on the *BMEWS* contract. In fact most, if not all members of the team worked on *BMEWS*.

The team's primary mission was to develop proposals for any new business within RCA Service Company. Typically the Corporate Contracts organization would obtain an RFP (Request for Proposal) requesting RCA to bid on a contract for new business. The Contracts Organization would evaluate the request and decide if the company should proceed or pass on the request. If the decision was to proceed they would select any team members they felt could contribute to the proposed Proposal. A typical team would generally consist of ten to twelve persons.

The location of where the proposed customer was located, would determine where the Team would develop the Proposal. If the customer was within driving distance, then the proposal was developed in Riverton NJ. Frequently, they would rent a small motel, all of it, and stay right there, using the empty rooms for office space. For example they developed a Proposal for the Army at the Presidio right at the south end of the Golden Gate Bridge at one time. That was a large proposal and it took them nearly three weeks to complete, however generally they would only be away from home for a week or ten days.

In about 1963 (the dates are beginning to get a little fuzzy) RCA received a notice from NASA at Goddard Space Flight Center to submit a proposal to operate their VERY large warehouse, located in Baltimore Md. This warehouse supported nearly one hundred RADAR Tracking stations located around the world whose sole purpose was to support the Apollo Space Missions.

Needless to say RCA was eventually awarded the contract however the road to getting there was an incredible story.

Chapter Four

RCA/NASA CONNECTION

In about 1963 (the dates are beginning to get a little fuzzy) RCA received an invitation from NASA at Goddard Space Flight Center to attend a Bid Conference at Goddard. The purpose was to invite interested Corporations to submit proposals/ bids to operate their VERY large warehouse located in Baltimore Md. This warehouse supplied everything from Kotex to complete radars for nearly one hundred RADAR Tracking stations, located around the world; all in the support of the Apollo Space Missions. The contract at that time was being operated by the Bendix Corporation.

RCA eventually won the contract; however it was an incredible journey getting there, so incredible in fact that it remains a very vivid memory to this very day. In response to the NASA request RCA sent a very strong delegation to the Bid Conference at Goddard Space Flight Center, located in Bethesda, Maryland to include: RCA Executive Vice President of Government Services whom we will call Mr. Rogers; Executive Vice President of the RCA Computer Division whom we will call Mr. Jones; the BMEWS Contract Manager whom we will call Mr. Vincent, and the Leader of the new Contract Proposal Team whom we will call Mr. Roberts.

At the Bid Conference it was revealed by NASA that they had recently spent over a million dollars of your hard earned taxes to have an outside consulting firm study the Warehouse Operation and develop detailed system specifications for the operation of that facility.

It was further revealed that these requirements and specifications were the basis for the current RFP (Request For proposal).

The above mentioned study had also determined the operation would require a very sophisticated on-line computer system that provided both real time updates and reporting (inquiries) and would dictate the investment of *huge amounts of money and resources* for compliance.

It was reported through the grapevine that a tentative decision had been made by the attending delegation on the way home from the bid conference to NO BID the contract as RCA could not or more realistically would not bid on the contract. That was about to change.

Dick has never had any specific information to confirm his suspicions, nor will he ever, since these people are now all gone; however if he were a betting man he would put his money on Mr. Roberts, the new Leader of the Proposal Team. Dick would further bet the discussion went something like this. "Look, we operate the BMEWS contract and have since its beginning. The logistics portion of that contract is at least ten times larger than this contract therefore; I have a plan on how we can bid this contract".

This was the PLAN. First, RCA has a large computer center that supports BMEWS, and has for many years however it lacks the real time access features that their RFQ requires. We would take our system, without the real time access and modify it to meet all of their requirements. We would further make all necessary changes to that system at no cost to NASA. This argument was so convincing that the above mentioned decision makers reversed their decision and RCA did positively respond to NASA's RFP.

Now that the decision had been made it was time for Dick to get involved. His first assignment, as a member of this team, was to review the RFP in detail, and determine what changes needed to be made to meet EACH and EVERY requirement. That was a full three or four day task and was completed over a weekend plus an additional couple of days. It immediately became clear that modifications to existing programs were not an option, but rather a complete rewrite would be required. The proposal did not indicate a rewrite would be necessary.

There was a Manual in the logistics business that needs to be addressed since it will appear frequently in virtually all discussions relating to logistics. Mr. Roberts, the Leader of the New Proposal Team was an old Air Force Supply Sargent and virtually all contracts relating to Logistics would include a reference to Air Force Logistics Manual AFM 67-1. That was the bible for all Logistic activities on ALL contracts.

After the review of the RFP was complete it was now time to begin writing the proposal. The two writers in this case were Mr. Roberts and one of his assistants. Dick would also like to point out another interesting fact. All members of the team were ex-military, starting with Mr. Vincent, retired Navy Captain; Mr. Roberts, former Air Force Logistics Sergeant; The second proposal writer, a former Air Force Captain; and Dick, a former Air Force Meteorologist Sergeant.

Writing the Logistics portion of the proposal was a monumental task that took a full ten days to complete because they addressed every requirement and specifically every change that was required. This is where Dick's earlier review became critical. Based on that review Dick used a black board to define each and every change that was required and the two writers converted that information into text.

Within about ten days the proposal was complete, including pricing and the complete proposed staffing. The staffing was:

Project Manager Mr. Roberts.

Dick Palmer would be proposed as Manager of Computer Development and Operations.

The remainder of the staff has not, nor will it be addressed in this story, but included such positions as: Finance, Personnel, Material Control, Engineering, and Quality Control, to name a few.

It was now time to submit the completed proposal back to NASA for final evaluation. At this point "DESTINY" once again took over. The word Destiny has several different meanings therefore Dick will define which definition that he has been referring to each and every time in this writing. When Dick uses the term "Destiny" he is referring to the direction of events that is contrary to the direction of events that most sane people would expect. In this case the probability of RCA winning this particular contract was virtually non-existent because they submitted a proposal completely contrary to the RFP requirements. A week or so passed and RCA was invited to attend a phase of the bidding process that is commonly referred to as "The Orals". This process is generally attended by top Management, plus some of the designated management team for the project. They are invited to sit with selected members of the proposal issuing committee to answer and/or clarify any responses that may be ambiguous. RCA's day (in court so to speak) was the day before Thanksgiving, 1963. At

1300 hours (1 PM) thru 1500 hours (3PM). Now Dick will describe the setting.

The meeting was conducted in a very large auditorium located at Goddard Space Flight Center that was filled to capacity with NASA employees (Dick assumed) from Goddard to carry on the inquisition. Every seat was filled so Dick further assumed it was for the purpose of adding to the intimidation factor. In addition there was numerous small radio microphones scattered throughout the auditorium that could be passed to anyone wanting to ask a question. Dick had never seen anything like those before as they looked like small flashlights.

The RCA team members were marched onto the stage, facing the audience. RCA had been directed to bring twelve participants, all identified in the proposal and all seated at a long table that stretched across the stage. In front of each participant was a Name Tag that identified you and your proposed management position, plus a microphone.

Once seated at the table you could get a better look at your surroundings. On the auditorium floor directly in front of the stage was a podium for the Director of Goddard Space Flight Center (GSFC) who would conduct the inquisition. Seated beside the director was a Court Recorder with her little recording machine.

Looking above the crowd, behind the top row of seats, was a very large recording studio all enclosed in glass that would record every word that was spoken. The recording media was two large reels of magnetic tape, each reel being an estimated two plus feet in diameter.

Now on the stage were the twelve RCA employees starting on the left as you faced the stage were; RCA Executive Vice President, Mr.

Rogers, followed to his left by the proposed Contract Manager, Mr. Roberts and to his left was, Mahlon Palmer, proposed Manager of Computer Operations and Development. The remaining nine to Dick's left were the rest of the Management Team as detailed in the proposal.

The meeting began with Mr. Rogers making an opening statement and then the fun began. It became immediately apparent the plan was to destroy us, since all questions were specifically directed towards a person who would obviously not know the answer, and then they would move on to the next question. For Dick a strange thing happened since he was only asked one question during the entire meeting, so the question was obviously why?

Incidentally, the question was about Finance and Dick obviously did not know the answer. The question remained, why no questions for the one person that was designated to be the Manager of all computer operations. Dick, at that time was also only about twenty-six years old, the youngest by far of anyone else sitting on the stage.

After about an hour Mr. Rogers requested a potty break and everyone went to the rest room. Before the RCA people even got inside of the rest room the place had filled up with NASA people, all asking questions. Finally everyone got back to the table and questioning again began in earnest. This time the meeting continued until about five PM. Once on their way home, it was unanimously agreed that NASA was not impressed with RCA'S alternative approach and they would never be heard from again.

Everyone got back to New Jersey and was very happy that a very long two or three week period of intensive work was finally over and that everyone was ready for the long Thanksgiving Day break.

Immediately following their return to work after the Thanksgiving break on Tuesday morning, RCA's Mr. Rogers received a phone call from NASA with a most unusual request. First they told Mr. Rogers that RCA's proposal was far and away the best proposal they received. They indicated they would like RCA to send a couple of their most knowledgeable people to Goddard Space Flight Center to meet with NASA's Director of all of NASA'S computer operations, worldwide, whom we will refer to as Doctor Smith. NASA had flown Dr. Smith in from Houston Space Flight Center for the express purpose of conducting this meeting. Dr. Smith would chair this meeting and he was surrounded by a group of probably some forty or more obviously high ranking individuals, most likely from Godard Space Flight Center.

Dr. Smith indicated that he and his associates had a series of in-depth questions regarding our proposal and the associated software. Since Mr. Roberts and Dick Palmer had done virtually all of the work on putting the proposal together, they were the obvious choice to go to this meeting.

The meeting was scheduled for all day on Thursday so Mr. Roberts and Dick got an early start to be sure they got there on time. They also travelled with a great deal of apprehension due to the treatment they had received just a week before. They were immediately introduced to Doctor Smith as the Chief Honcho of all computer activities throughout ALL of NASA.

Doctor Smith was going to moderate this meeting and suggested either Mr. Roberts or Dick go to the blackboard and the other go to the back of the room. Since Dick already had a great deal of experience at the blackboard, particularly in the development of this proposal, Mr. Roberts suggested that he once again go to the board.

The room was filled with probably fifty or sixty predominately men that we believed to be managers of the various operations; however, after the first two or three questions Dick quickly concluded that the gallery was all or nearly all PHD's brought there specifically to get to the bottom of everything. Your next question should probably be why Dick suspected they were all PHD's. Over the years Dick had interfaced with numerous PHD's and most all exhibit similar and unique characteristics. First they are usually extremely knowledgeable about most all aspects of their particular branch of study, however, once out of their realm that knowledge base diminishes rapidly. They almost always stand before speaking, possibly to insure everyone knows who is speaking. Once they begin to speak they begin to pontificate, frequently about irrelevant information. These traits must be learned during their many years of college since they almost always exhibit the same pattern.

Doctor Smith essentially asked all the questions, with very little input from the gallery. He asked very specific questions about many of RCA's proposed solutions to what would become contractual requirements. One question that received a great deal of attention was the location of RCA's computer processing facility. RCA had proposed placing a large computer center in Westminster Maryland where RCA owned Random House Books and where all processing would take place. If you remember RCA DID NOT propose direct on-line access for updates and inquiries as required by the RFP. As RCA later found out they did not receive a single proposal that met those requirements. In essence NASA was looking for a 2010 solution in the 1960's using technology that was not even available in that time frame.

As a similarity, remember the debacle the government attempted in the 2013-2014 time frame called Health Care (ObamaCare) and the hundreds of millions of dollars spent without success.

In any event the meeting continued until well into the afternoon with them apparently convinced we really did know what we were talking about. On the way home (back to New Jersey) Mr. Roberts and Dick concluded the meeting had gone well, in fact very well.

Within two or three days RCA again heard from NASA and this time they were asking for a demonstration of our system. Mr. Robert's came by Dick's office to break the news. Dick's immediate response was I hope you have some great ideas since, you know there *ain't no* system. Dick was left by himself to ponder the problem. Dick's first step was to call Mr. Rogers and seek guidance. In fact Dick's comment was "you know there is no system so there is nothing to demonstrate". His response was, "it's up to you, figure it out" and thus ended the conversation.

RCA had a large computer center in the corporate headquarters building located in Cherry Hill, NJ and this is where the *DEMONSTRATION* would take place. Let me try to describe the setting. The Center was the show piece of the company and was in an all glass enclosure just as you entered the building. The computer was the largest Spectra 70/45 computer that they made and it was surrounded by probably 25-30 magnetic tape drives along the outside wall. RCA also had the industry's fastest printer that would print three thousand lines per minute. Add to that a very high speed card reader and punch.

The demonstration was scheduled for the Sunday afternoon just before Christmas. NASA showed up with a large bus full of people from Goddard Space Flight Center under the guidance of the Director of Goddard Space Flight Center. Many of these attendees were the same PHD's that had participated in the meeting in Goddard just a few days before. All attendees gathered outside the glass enclosure and waited for the demonstration to begin. The NASA gathering was entertained by: VP Mr. Rogers, VP Mr. Jackson, Manager to be Mr. Vincent and Mr. Roberts.

Dick was in the computer room and began the demonstration with a large tape sort that ran for probably 30-40 minutes. For those unfamiliar with the term "Tape Sort" let me try to explain. First of all, tape drives are virtually non-existent in today's world, having been replaced by much faster random access devices, however with over a dozen of these devices jumping up and down it left a very significant impression. While the sort was running one of Dick's assistants ran a couple thousand cards through the high speed card reader and another assistant punched a thousand cards or so using the high speed card punch. Dick had previously mounted a tape that contained several computer generated print files and they were now ready for show and tell.

Finally the sort was complete so Dick went outside where all of NASA guests and RCA management were waiting and advised them that processing was complete and invited them into the computer room. Dick further suggested they should gather around the printer where they could better view the results. Little did they know this printer was so fast that printed reports would stand paper over two feet tall before cascading over the back. They looked at a couple of the reports and they were totally convinced they had seen the total system that RCA had proposed and it suddenly had appeared before their eyes.

They never realized they had seen **absolutely nothing** that they came for except a pretty good demonstration of RCA's computer performance. As a thought, this had to be the second Biggest Hoax in NASA history with Apollo 11 ranking NUMBER 1, (in my opinion).

A few days later Mr. Rogers stopped by Dick's office to tell him they had signed a contract with NASA that included everything as written. The contract was worth a mere $43 million dollars. Mr. Roger's comment was "You sold it, now you can go build it" and thus it was so.

Shortly after the contract was signed and Dick had been identified as the Manager of all computer operations on the contract, it was time to move to Baltimore. That move would occur during the spring of 1966 and that first year would prove to be very hectic. Part of the deal was that Dick would assume total responsibility for all detail design of the new system as well as hire personnel to fill all key positions to include; two or three programmers, a Leader for the Key Punch Operation as well as a Leader of the rest of the operation. The most important position that needed to be filled as quickly as possible was the Lead Programmer that would assume total responsibility for the development of the single most important program in the entire operation. The person that Dick selected was a Programmer whom we will refer to as John Brown and he would remain on the contract until the very end. Just a note about John, he was also ex-military and he had been stationed in Turkey during the same time that Dick was there. Dick on the other hand needed to spend nearly all his time on designing the new system since RCA had a contractual obligation to have the system Fully Operational by January 1, 1967.

About this time Dick and Joy had a major interruption at their new home in Baltimore. They actually moved into their new House (new to them) on the NW side of Baltimore in April 1966. Less than one month later on Friday May 13th their house was struck by lightning at about 10:30 PM at night. This house was a typical Cape Cod with a kitchen, dining room, living room and bedroom on the lower floor. The upstairs had two rooms, one considerably larger than the other, plus a full bath. They used the larger room as a Den where they had their TV plus Dick's rather extensive book collection. Joy also had many Knick Knacks in that room.

The Living Room had a large fireplace on one end with a large mirror resting on the mantle. The mirror stretched across the mantle from side to side, and from the mantle to the ceiling. With the large fireplace on the inside, there was an equally large chimney on the outside. The chimney above the roof was about four feet wide, some eighteen inches front to back and extended some five or six feet above the roof. The actual lightning strike chose this chimney as its primary target. The house sat back from the street some one hundred to one hundred fifty feet and the top three feet of the chimney was 'carefully' placed in the center of the street by the lightning strike.

Immediately following the strike Dick could smell ozone so he went upstairs to check for damage. When he opened a closet door he could immediately see the entire roof above the large room was all on fire. Dick gave Joy a shout and told her to call the Fire Department. Fortunately she had noticed a FIRE CALL box almost at the end of their driveway and called the Fire Department from there. The Baltimore County Volunteer Fire Department responded almost immediately.

What Dick is about to tell you now was absolutely amazing. Three fire trucks pulled up in front of the house on the street, accompanied by 60-70 firemen. The center truck was carrying three large flood lights mounted on it, thus the front yard was like daylight (Remember the time was now approaching midnight). Six firemen came to the front door, opened it without destruction and came into the house. Three firemen went upstairs and three remained on the first floor. The ones downstairs moved all furniture to the center of each room and covered it with tarps. We were not allowed upstairs so I cannot describe the activity up there. Finally around 1:30 AM the firemen were ready to leave after they told us we could stay there for the night.

After their departure Joy and Dick decide to go upstairs to see if they could at least salvage a part of Dick's books. What they found was absolutely unbelievable. The firemen had removed nearly all of the ceiling along with all of the insulation above it in that room. In addition, much of the roof in that part of the house had been destroyed and removed, and then the firemen placed a large tarp over the big hole in the roof to keep any rain out of the house.

Moving back downstairs the big mirror above the fireplace was now just a clear piece of glass and much of the ceiling paint in the living room had been vaporized. Directly above where Dick had been standing at the time of the strike was a large hole blown into the ceiling. Most of the tiles on the bathroom walls were shattered and much of the electrical wiring throughout the entire house needed to be replaced. The chimney suffered major damage, both inside and out and appeared to have been hit by a huge shotgun blast.

Apart from the structural damage they had *ABSOLUTELY* no water damage or any other damage caused by the firemen. In fact after the firemen left you literally could not even tell they had been there.

The next morning when Dick called the insurance adjuster, the first words he said when he walked into the house was "Baltimore County Volunteers were here last night. How do you know that, Dick asked? He said if the city had been here last night the front door would have been smashed and every window would have been shattered. His comment was, "a fire to them is just another opportunity to have fun".

There were extensive repairs required to get the house back in shape; however in time everything returned to normal. Joy had to take care of the house pretty much by herself since Dick was working most of the time.

By the time the house was back in order we were well into the fall and time was beginning to run out on meeting our contractual requirements with our implementation deadline of January 1st fast approaching. After meeting our contractual requirements there were many opportunities to improve how sites were required to operate and that was next on the agenda.

When RCA took over the contract all one hundred or so sites around the world submitted their orders for parts/supplies by teletype that required they be keypunched before processing. The first major change that RCA implemented was to receive those orders on paper tape directly from the teletype thus eliminating the expense and delay of keypunching. This was a huge improvement.

Another contractual requirement was to publish and distribute a complete catalog consisting of over one thousand pages each month to every site. These catalogs were required to be printed on the computer, made into books and then shipped all over the world.

After much research Dick discovered their contract had a VECP (Value Engineering Change Proposal) clause that they could use to change the contract. Essentially these clauses encouraged a contractor to propose changes to a contract that would improve the performance of the contract while at the same time saving money. Generally the contractor and the government would share the savings on a 50/50 basis. RCA actively pursued these changes and encouraged their employees to submit ideas. Generally the employee would receive $25 for each proposal submitted, and if the proposal was accepted and implemented the employee would receive ten percent of RCA's share up to a total of $10,000.

Dick suggested that this catalog be produced and distributed on microfiche, thus saving the printing and distribution cost of this monster catalog each month. For this idea he received the maximum award of $10,000.

By this time the contract was operating smoothly and everyone was beginning to get excited about the upcoming Apollo 11 mission. The Director of Goddard Space Flight Center had personally invited the RCA Team to visit Goddard Space Flight Center during the mission and witness the operation from inside Mission Control. Three or four of the team, including Dick, accepted the invitation to take advantage of the opportunity.

Mission Control was like a large amphitheater with many seats and nearly dark with virtually no lights. The area where a stage would normally be located was filled with numerous large consoles, with many flashing lights and two or three technicians at each console. The console area was dimly lit. The experience was so exciting Dick nearly wet himself, but instead he took a nap. Dick also had an opportunity to visit the same for Apollo 12 but passed. He must admit there was not much to see.

July 4th 1971 provided the next opportunity for a unique experience. July 4th that year occurred on Monday, thus giving everyone a long three day weekend so Dick and Joy were going to visit Dick's family in upstate New York. Trying to leave Baltimore on Friday afternoon on a long weekend was insane so their plan was to get some sleep early in the evening, then depart sometime after midnight when there would be virtually no traffic. The plan was sound. Traffic on the Baltimore Beltway was almost nonexistent. As usual they turned north on Interstate 83 heading towards York, Pa. They had a relatively new car (1966 Chevrolet I believe) and the weather was very hot, therefore they were driving with the windows down. Dick was driving and there was not a single car on the road, nor had there been since getting on I-83. Since there was NO traffic Dick had the car on cruise at 65 MPH.

This was a road that they had travelled many times. Incidentally I-83 at that time was four lanes wide, two lanes north and two lanes south, the lanes being divided by thick woods so it was impossible to see south bound traffic. Suddenly off to the northwest and to the left of the road Dick noticed a slowly flashing red light that was consistent with radio towers of that time however this one he had never noticed before. Dick mentioned his observation to Joy and she agreed she did not remember any towers in that area either. Suddenly the light began to move slowly eastward towards I-83. The flashing red light was now directly over I-83 AND DIRECTLY ABOVE THE CAR when suddenly an intensely bright light came on and stayed directly above the car for up to a mile. *THERE WAS NOT A SINGLE CAR ANY PLACE ON THE ROAD.* Suddenly a car appeared in the rear view mirror that had just rounded a bend probably a mile distant. As soon as that car appeared the light went out. Dick immediately pulled off the road and got out of the car. The object, whatever it was, made no noise and had no distinguishing features, except the little flashing red light and it was flying just above the treetops. It was also headed directly towards Baltimore when it suddenly made a ninety degree turn to the right, then disappeared behind the trees. After they got their pants cleaned up a bit they continued their journey north to New York without further incident.

This was during the time when many people were reporting UFO's and were accused of being crazy. They did not discuss this incident for many years however this story is now registered in the UFO Museum in Roswell, New Mexico. Interestingly while at the UFO Museum they met an old sheep farmer who had a very similar experience on his ranch in New Mexico. A number of years ago Mary and Dick were watching Unsolved Mysteries on TV when they had a segment about a State Trooper in Ohio who had the exact same experience, except his car stopped and would not restart until the light went out. They had no answers either.

Chapter Five

RCA/GREENLAND CONNECTION

In about 1971 RCA received notification that the BMEWS contract would be going out for bid again. It had been some three to four years ago that RCA had lost it, however this time the contract would include the DEW Line which was another large contract. The DEW Line, for those unfamiliar with the term, was a line of radars that extended from the very west coast of Alaska, across the northern coast of Alaska, across northern Canada, across Greenland and down into Iceland. Its mission was to identify and track *any aircraft* that was approaching both Canada and the United States from Russia over the North Pole. There were probably some twenty to twenty-five sites in all.

For those unfamiliar with BMEWS (Ballistic Missile Early Warning System) it was a large contract that operated two large RADARS built specifically to track any Russian ballistic missiles that are approaching the United States from over the North Pole. This particular contract included a site in the very northern part of Greenland, near Thule AFB and a second site at Clear, Alaska near Fairbanks. A third BMEWS site is located in Burton Wood, England; however that site was not part of this contract.

This was a most fortuitous event for many RCA employees that had just become available from the NASA Contract, with these two new contracts going to be administered out of Ent Air Force Base, located in Colorado Springs, Colorado. RCA had decided to create a small subsidiary company that would employ all regular employees that worked on the contract; however all of top management would remain with the RCA Service Company Headquartered in Colorado Springs, Colorado.

The President of the new company was from Cherry Hill, with others such as Finance, Personnel, and Contracts etc. were from many different businesses. Those moving to Colorado Springs from Baltimore were: Mr. Roberts, Assistant to the President, Mahlon (Dick) Palmer, Manager of Logistics Services and Mr. Snyder, Supervisor of Computer Operations.

The Manager of Logistics Services had a very broad range of responsibilities as you will see. Following is a list of Departments that reported directly to Dick and what their responsibilities were. Fortunately he had a very large pool of retired military to choose from and they were all rated as the best of the best in their career field throughout the Air Force.

Logistics Documentation

Fuels Management

Third Party Management

Food Service Management

Sealift Coordinator

Computer Center Management

Before Dick goes further he should give you a little history about the two separate and distinct missions of both BMEWS and the

DEW Line and describe the areas where they were located. BMEWS (Ballistic Missile Early Warning System) was originally conceived and building began sometime in the mid to late 1950's (I believe) to locate, track and identify Russian missiles approaching the US and Canada from over the North Pole. BMEWS as originally conceived consisted of three sites, one being located in Greenland at Thule Air Base, and more precisely at the J Site some twenty to thirty miles north of Thule Air Force Base which is located in the very northern reaches of Greenland. A second major site was located in Alaska and was built some 75 miles northwest of Fairbanks in the village of Clear and a third and final site was located in Burton Wood, England. Note: Having worked on the BMEWS project for more than five years, at two different times, this is the only site Dick never visited.

The two sites at Clear and Thule were similar; the major difference was the site at Thule had four large directional radars with fixed non movable and concaved radar screens that were approximately 400 feet long and an estimated 160 plus feet high, whereas the site at Clear only had three of these same type of directional radars. It was rumored at the time that these large radars could locate and track an object the size of a basketball at 25,000 miles. What was their real capability? We'll never know. These RADARS produced a tremendous amount of energy as evidenced by the fact if a bird, any kind of bird, flew through the radar beam they were instantly cooked and fell to earth. Each site also had a single one hundred sixty foot diameter tracking RADAR. On one of Dick's visits to Thule he was given a tour of the tracking RADOME that turned out to be quite an experience. First a little information about how these sites worked. The fixed screen radars were constantly scanning the skies for ANY activity that was known or unknown. Once an object was detected the tracking RADAR was activated by giving it a search window to locate and identify the object. Tracking continued until the object was positively identified. If the object was not positively identified many highly classified actions were initiated. Every known object in space, even junk was cataloged and identified for verification.

During this particular visit inside the dome an object was identified by the directional RADAR which in turn activated the tracking RADAR. Now Dick will tell you a little about the inside of the dome. First, remember the dish was 160 feet in diameter, thus the dome must be somewhat larger. Now imagine a three foot wide cat walk all the way around the domes' greatest diameter.

Suddenly while standing on that cat walk minding his own business, try to visualize this 160 foot monster coming to life as it moves directly over the top in an arc of 180 degrees, then going into search mode consisting of ever smaller circles as it searches for the identified object. All of this activity occurred within five seconds or less. Your immediate reaction is to get out of the way when you quickly realize "Da Ain't No Place To Go".

Once the object is located and verified the dish automatically returns to its normal resting position. You might ask what happens if the object cannot be verified. Quite frankly Dick has no idea. Each BMEWS site had a single tracking radar with a dish of about 160 feet in diameter.

The DEW (Defensive Early Warning) Line Contract was much larger, cost wise; because it physically spanned a much larger area. The DEW Line was originally conceived maybe during the late 40's but certainly no later than the 50's with the primary purpose of locating and tracking low flying aircraft approaching Canada and the United States from Russia over the North Pole. Keep in mind missiles at that time were not nearly as highly developed as they are now, thus much less risk.

There was a major DEW Line Site at Soderstrum, Greenland which is located some two hours flying time south of Thule and this site supported all the DEW Line sites in Greenland. These sites included two sites on the ice cap, one on the eastern coast of Greenland and one or more sites on the western coast of Greenland.

There were at least five primary sites strategically spaced across northern Canada and Alaska, each supporting several minor sites and they were named: Dye Main, Fox Main and Cambridge Bay. There were two more main sites in Alaska, those being Barter Island located on an island just off the Alaska/Canadian border and the final site at Point Barrow, Alaska. This site had responsibility for all the remainder of the Alaskan sites along the northern coast to the western coast of Alaska.

All but three of all the sites on both contracts had deep water ports that were used to supply them with food, fuel and any other materials that they needed during what was known as the Summer Sealift. The other three sites required all of their supplies to be flown in.

Dick's very first task upon arriving in Colorado Springs was to fill the management positions on his staff. Those positions have been previously stated. Fortunately for both Dick, and RCA, he had a very large pool of highly qualified candidates, located in Colorado Springs, all recently retired and available for hire. Many of these candidates had held these exact same positions in the military while they were on active duty.

First, Dick hired two retired Chief Master Sergeants, both rated number 1 and number 2 respectively within all of the Air Force, and they had complete control of everything relating to fuels all across the Artic. Their responsibilities included; fuel spills, contaminated fuel, Quality Control, Inventory, etc. They also controlled many kinds of fuels such as DFA (Diesel Fuel Artic), Auto Fuel (Gasoline), numerous kinds of aircraft fuel, such as JP4, plus a number of classified fuels. In addition they had responsibility for all gasses such as oxygen and nitrogen. Each site had at least one fuels expert that reported (operationally) directly to this group.

The contracts Logistics Documentation coordinator was responsible for ensuring that all Logistics procedures were current and being followed at all sites including BMEWS and the DEW Line. He also coordinated the distribution of all changes and assured their timely Implementation. This position was filled by a Retired Full Colonel.

The Food Service coordinator was responsible for everything relating to food on both the BMEWS and DEW Line contracts. For example, he was responsible for developing the master menus for every site, ensuring that every person was receiving the specified calories each day. As Dick remembers, every person was to be allotted at least 5000 calories each day to compensate for the extreme cold weather. Then using the projected manning for the coming year, the food requirements for each site was calculated so that the necessary food could be purchased in preparation for the summer sealift. The sealift only included nonperishable food since basically, all perishable food was flown into each site on a weekly basis. This position was filled by a Retired Senior Master Sergeant

So you may wonder where the perishable food actually came from. RCA operated essentially three large buying facilities that purchased that food and they were located in Anchorage, Alaska, Winnipeg, Canada and southern New Jersey for the Greenland sector.

Third Party Coordinator: Any person *not* permanently stationed at one of the sites was considered a Third Party, therefore there was a requirement to know where they were at all times, insure they had food and shelter, and insure they had the proper clearances for their approved activities, etc.

Sealift Coordinator. This person was responsible for the coordination of all activities relating to the Summer/Winter Sea Lifts. The Summer Sea Lift was an extremely critical operation due to the very short season when it MUST BE COMPLETED. Any miscalculation could and occasionally did result in a ship getting frozen into the ice for the winter. Once in a great while, if the ship was critical to the operation, the Navy would send in an Ice Breaker and try to free the ship, but normally it just remained frozen in the ice until the following summer.

As large as the operation was, the whole Sea Lift went extremely well each year due to meticulous and precise planning. In addition to the Summer Sealift, they also had a Winter Air Lift that was completed entirely by air. There were three small sites in northern Canada that were landlocked, thus everything needed to be flown in. Each site had a short dirt runway that could handle small aircraft, but nothing the size needed to bring in all the fuel, food and all the other stuff needed for the year. This task was relegated to the much larger C-130 Hercules aircraft flown by the Air Force.

So the next logical question would be where did they land? Each of these sites were located very close to a large lake, large enough to accept the C-130; however the C-130 could only land on these lakes when the ice was a minimum of sixty inches (60 inches) thick. Therefore all flying must be done when the average temperatures were at least 50 degrees below zero. Even with sixty inches of ice, the ice would buckle and needed to be smoothed. Smoothing was accomplished by pumping water from the lake below and letting it refreeze.

Computer Center Operation: The final organization that fell under the management of the Logistics Services organization was operation of a relatively large Computer Center. The center was designed around the largest RCA Spectra 70/45 Computer with both tape and direct access devices. It had the other classic computer center functions which included: computer operations, system development and data entry functionality.

With such a wide span of control one would logically expect much travel, and so it was. There was almost always someone and many times two or three people up on the line most of the time.

Travel was not easy due to the large area that they supported; therefore Dick will try to discuss the various major sectors. They were: Greenland Sector, Iceland Sector, Dye Main Sector (eastern Canada), Fox Main Sector (Eastern Central Canada), Cambridge Bay Sector (Western Central Canada), Barter Island Sector (area surrounding the Alaska/Canada Border) and finally the Point Barrow

Sector (That Sector included all of the remaining sites along the Alaskan Coast Line). Incidentally, Point Barrow is the most northern point of the continental United States.

All travel to the Greenland and Icelandic sectors always originated from McGuire Air Force base in central New Jersey with typically one flight per week; therefore your shortest trip would be one week long. The aircraft generally used for those flights was the old workhorse Boeing 727 and during most of the time while working on this contract, that airline was operated by Braniff.

Generally all travel within Canada and frequently into eastern Alaska departed from Winnipeg with a destination of Cambridge Bay or Fox Main, flying on a Boeing 737. Again there was one flight per week alternating between the two sites. In fact Dick once sent one of his guys up there for one week and it took an additional five weeks to get him back home. Actually, it got so bad this guy finally flew home commercially down through Fairbanks.

Generally travel in Alaska was very dependent on where you were going. For example, if you were going to the DEW Line (in other words up on the northern coast) you may fly into Fairbanks, or you may be sent up through Winnipeg. On the other hand if you were going to the BMEWS site at Clear you would fly into Fairbanks, and then take the bus to Clear. In any case it was a full day's journey.

There was a contractual requirement that at least once every two months the contractor must schedule an inspection flight primarily for the Air Force to visit any sites they chose. Also, these trips averaged approximately two weeks in duration. Dick's organization had a contractual requirement to have at least one member on every flight and if there were any Air Force personnel above the rank of Captain on the flight then the Manager of the Logistics Service Organization (Dick) must be on the flight. The code name for this flight was affectionately referred to as the ARTIC STAR. Trust me; people were not waiting in line to take the ride, therefore Dick set up a policy that every Manager in his organization would need to take their scheduled turn.

A typical trip would begin at Ent Air Force Base with the issuance of your Artic Gear, to include; Parka, Gloves, Artic Boots, Sleeping Bag, etc., with your name clearly affixed to the outside. This was your most precious commodity and stayed with you *wherever* you went. Keep in mind the environment that you could be subjected to could include temperatures of 60 to 65 degrees below zero and winds in excess of 100 MPH.

The appointed time for departure would finally arrive with the plane fully loaded. Generally the first stop would be in Winnipeg for an overnight, with a visit to RCA facilities, particularly their buying facility that purchased all perishable food used throughout the Canadian Sector. Each trip was different and was based on Air Force requirements for that trip. However to give you a flavor of a typical trip Dick will give you what a typical scenario would be like. From Winnipeg the next stop would usually be Anchorage, Alaska (another buying Facility), or Fairbanks, Alaska if a major visit was scheduled for the large BMEWS site at Clear. Clear was generally a two or three hour bus ride from the airport to the site where you would remain over Night (RON). The following day the procedure would be reversed and you would be on your way to the next stop. Essentially this same procedure would be followed for two consecutive weeks (no wonder no one wanted to take the trip). These trips generally made stops all across Alaska, Canada, and Greenland. Rarely if ever, did these trips go to Iceland or out onto the Greenland icecap due to the size of the plane.

Since we are talking about the fun trip called the Artic Star, Dick will tell you a little story about an adventure that occurred on one of those fun trips. The adventure began innocently enough with a short stop at one of the very remote sites in western Canada, near the Alaskan /Canadian border. The site was very small, with probably less than ten men stationed there. There were the usual approximately twenty plus men on board the F-227 aircraft (the standard aircraft used for the Artic Star trips).

Suddenly, the weather began to deteriorate, and the pilots were notified that the weather had begun to deteriorate rapidly at their final destination of FOX Main in the northerly center of Canada, on the northern shore line. The pilots were advised they should depart their present location and proceed post haste to their final destination. As has previously been stated, when Dick was flying while up on the line, he was almost always allowed to fly in the jump seat up in the cockpit and such was the case on this trip.

It is now time to describe the site of FOX Main in a bit more detail. Fox Main had a particular feature that was unique to only that one site. This site had two very large TROPO Antennas for the sole purpose of communicating with the outside world to the south. It is very hard to describe these antennas; however they looked somewhat like a very large *pair* of shoe horns sitting upside down. Each antenna was certainly more than one hundred feet tall and proportionally as wide. They were also concave top to bottom and side to side. In essence, they were very unique.

As they approached the site, those two TROPO antennas were the only objects that were protruding above the severe ground blizzards, with maybe only about half of them visible above the blowing snow. Everything else about the site was obliterated. For all of you pilots, the answer is no, they had no approach beacons or navigational aids of any kind. Also up there (AT THAT TIME), alternate airports were not even an option (there were none within one hundred plus miles). In essence, you play the hand you are dealt.

So what to do? The pilot stated that he knew the runway was located to the south of the TROPO'S, therefore he would go out over the ocean where there was open water AND no blowing snow. Once there he could drop down to about one hundred feet or so and then he started to make his approach in an attempt to find the runway. Great plan; one minor problem. Suddenly, directly in front of the aircraft was an open hanger door, with NO opening on the other side. So what to do? Travelling at probably 60-70 knots, the pilot JAMMED the power to full throttle and gently eased that baby over the roof. Dick didn't have time to check but he suspects there may have been tire marks on the hanger roof.

After finding the hanger on the first approach it was time to make a second attempt, only a little further south of the TROPS's. The second attempt was a success with missing the end of the runway by maybe a hundred feet. Those pilots up on the DEW Line were phenomenal as Dick is sure that was just another day in the office.

There is another interesting aspect of this story; those twenty or so guys in the back of the plane never knew how close they came to meeting their maker. Dick can tell you it was close, very close.

As can be seen, much of our time was spent travelling to and from the Artic. Once at a site, you were generally there for a minimum of one week and many times depending on the weather you were there for much longer; therefore Dick will now tell you about a few adventures that he had an opportunity to become a part of. On one visit to Soderstrum, Greenland the weather had been extremely bad for nearly thirty days and no aircraft had been able to fly into either of the two DEW Line Sites that were situated on the Greenland Ice Cap. Those two sites could only be reached by the large four engine C-130 aircraft that were fitted with skis. Normally, the wind chill was required to be above 40 or 50 degrees *below* zero, however since there had been no aircraft into one of the sites for so long they decided to make an exception to go in with the wind chills much below established minimums.

Usually whenever flying up on the line, even in the Air Force C130 again Dick was almost always allowed to fly in the jump seat up with the aircrew and this trip was no exception. Before we get too far into the story the two sites on the Greenland Ice cap were located at an elevation in excess of 12,000 feet (atop thousands of feet of solid ice). The outbound trip to the site was uneventful and when we landed they immediately began to unload the aircraft. As usual Dick had his trusty camera with him to take advantage of any photo opportunities that might present themselves. Keep in mind by this time the wind chill was in the 60/70 degree below zero range and by the time Dick was able to get the camera out of his parka he had time to take exactly one photo before the camera completely froze. Fortunately he was able to get one outstanding photo.

After lunch and a quick look around the site it was time to leave. With the C-130 loaded and the engines running it was time to taxi out to the runway and get ready for takeoff. But wait, did someone talk about a runway? There was no runway since when you are out on the ice cap you have an Omni directional runway where everything is runway. After the run-up was complete it was now time for takeoff. But wait again, this time the skis were frozen solid to the ice cap. The pilot turned around and with a wink and a nod and the word "Watch"; he revved all four engines to max RPM and put both engines on one side of the plane full forward and both engines on the opposite side in full reverse and twisted that big sucker right out of its vise grip hold and the plane immediately became free and away we went. So much for another day in the balmy artic where the temperature was a mere 65 degrees below zero and the gentle breezes were hanging in at about sixty/seventy plus knots.

On one of those trips while flying across the eastern part of the DEW Line in the DYE sector, Dick was flying in the standard F-227 twin engine Fairchild plane with a load of cargo. The crew on the plane was the typical Pilot and Copilot plus crew chief/load master. As it was getting late it was time to find a place to stop for dinner and spend the night. Dick doesn't remember the exact site but it was one that only had six to ten men. When travelling alone like that you quickly make friends with anyone who will talk with you. So it was on this trip. The Crew chief and Dick quickly struck up a conversation as they ate their evening meal. Most sites had a small Day Room where you could relax, play cards, Ping-Pong or pool. This Day Room also had a piano. While setting there, Dick was chatting with his new friend when he started to hit single notes on the piano. Dick suggested he turn around and play if he liked, thus he did. What music he produced on that old clunker. Dick asked him what he really did for a living. He told Dick he was a Concert Pianist for the Montreal Philharmonic Orchestra and was just up on the Line for a little vacation. What an evening of music in a most unusual place.

The next day Dick was scheduled to leave Greenland but not to return home to Colorado for you see he still had a couple of adventures that needed more attention.

The plane ride back to McGuire AFB in the standard C-727 was uneventful as usual with arrival in the late evening as the time of year was January/February time frame. Dick nearly forgot to mention he was scheduled to immediately board another C-727 jet this time bound for Keflavik, Iceland for a weeklong stay there. The itinerary included a scheduled refueling stop in Goose bay, Labrador then on to Keflavik for arrival at around 0600 hours the next morning.

First, Dick must tell you when he travelled alone (which was nearly all the time) he always requested a window seat under the center engine in the very last row of the 727. This is statistically the safest seat on the plane. He was in his favorite seat.

As they were making their approach into Goose Bay, Dick suddenly realized their approach speed was much greater than normal. It is very hard to estimate air speed, particularly in the dark, however Dick was guessing their speed was 20/30 knots above normal, then when they touched down everything became crystal clear as the pilot slammed that sucker (plane) on the ground, followed by a panic stop. The winds were so strong it was almost impossible to taxi.

Finally they got the plane to the ramp area and got it secured. No one was allowed to deplane, not even during refueling which was very unusual. Finally, they boarded all the new passengers and prepared for departure. There was not a single empty seat available. Lest you forget there is nothing but a lot of cold water and icebergs between Goose Bay and Keflavik, particularly during January and February.

It was now time for the real FUN to begin. After a long and laborious taxi to the runway followed by the normal run-up activities it was time for departure. They taxied into position and began their take-off roll, unlike any that Dick had ever encountered before, but not the last. Just to refresh your memory about Dick's favorite seat on the 727 aircraft; window seat, last row in the aircraft, right under the number two engine, you know the big engine built right into the tail.

They began their takeoff roll and almost immediately the fun began. The cross wind was so strong it caused the number two engine (the one directly above Dick's head) to FLAME OUT momentarily, only to reignite a few moments later with a very loud explosion and the associated fire ball rolling down the runway. From Dick's vantage point he was able to witness several of those explosions. After what seemed like an eternity and after a significant number of those major explosions the take-off was aborted. The plane taxied back to the end of the runway and parked on the taxi strip apparently contemplating their next move.

After sitting on the taxi strip for some ten to fifteen minutes the plane began to roll slowly down the runway and EVERYONE was sure the take-off was being aborted. WRONG. The plane began to pick up speed, there were several more major fireballs and associated explosions AND THEY WERE AIRBORNE. Remember there isn't much between Goose Bay and Keflavik, Iceland in January except a lot of icy cold water. Dick should point out there was a tremendous amount of dirty underwear on the remainder of that flight. You could tell by the extremely foul smell throughout the plane.

After they got settled into their new home at Keflavik and Dick had a chance to talk to some of his local contacts they indicated the number two engine was completely destroyed and needed to be replaced before it could fly again. That was ok since Dick would not be leaving for at least a week.

Unfortunately Dick did not have time for any sightseeing, or at least not much while he was there but he did get a chance to get into Raycovick for a short visit with his host and family. There is much gorgeous scenery in Iceland and is a place Dick someday would hope to return. The return flight from Iceland to McGuire AFB in New Jersey was also uneventful.

Before we leave eastern Canada and the Dewline there is time for one more short story about flying in the Arctic. Very little is remembered about this particular trip except Dick was flying into DYE Main in the eastern sector of Canada where Dick would stop for a day or two. He had been flying on the standard F-227 aircraft which was the most common passenger aircraft used in that part of the contract. First Dick will give you a brief description of the aircraft. It was a twin engine turbo aircraft, and was frequently used to fly passengers. It also had one other interesting characteristic. Being of a high wing design, the landing gear was mounted in the engine nacelles, thus when on the ground its very long landing gear appeared like spider legs falling out of the wings.

Since Dick would be remaining overnight for a day or two, the aircraft would be departing after only a brief stop. Later, according to the official report, there had been much excitement aboard that aircraft shortly after departing for its final destination. As reported to Dick later that day, soon after they got into the air, the pilot got an indicator light signaling the door was not properly locked. First, it would be helpful to know where that door was located. The only door on the aircraft was located on the pilot side (left side) of the aircraft, directly in front of the left turbo prop engine, about three feet in front of that spinning prop. Fortunately, there was a big tough guy seated right next to the door and when the crew chief bent down to check the lock, the big guy would be holding the crew chief by the belt. At about that time the door flew open and the only thing that prevented the crew chief from going out, directly into that large spinning prop, was the big guy holding him by the belt. The door was now in the process of self-destructing while flopping, up and down in the wind. They landed post haste with everyone remaining overnight. That plane did not fly again for a very long period of time.

Before we leave Greenland and the Artic, Dick must tell you a little about the weather. You are certainly all familiar with blizzards with high winds and heavy snow in most anyplace in the US however in Greenland they have storms that are referred to as PHASES. There were three categories; Phase I, Phase II and Phase III. Dick will attempt to describe a Phase III since they were the worst. Winds could easily reach speeds in excess of 125 to 140 MPH and you literally could not see your hand that was just six inches in front of your face. Add to that, the temperature could/would reach 60 to 70 degrees BELOW zero with wind chills substantially below that. Any activity outside of a building was ABSOLUTELY FORBIDDEN. Short distances between two very close buildings were connected by ropes, just so you wouldn't get lost between them when travelling ten feet or less.

The main road between the Base and the BMEWS J-Site was dirt and there generally was no travel except by bus. In sections along the road there were small buildings generally referred to as PHASE

SHELTERS. These shelters were heated and contained enough food to keep fifteen or twenty people alive for a few days. Incidentally remaining in a vehicle, any vehicle of any kind during any PHASE was generally considered a death sentence. You see the wind was so strong it would literally drive the snow/ice right through the window and door seals and completely fill the vehicle with ice in minutes.

Dick has seen the wind so strong that those big 55 thousand barrel fuel tanks looked like they had been hit by a bulldozer if they were empty.

Midway through the term of the contract, probably sometime in the early 1970's the Danish government of Greenland contacted the US government and requested that the US put together a plan to remove much of the STUFF that had accumulated over the years during the construction and operation of Thule Air Force Base, the BMEWS radar site, Soderstrum Air Force Base and other Dew Line sites located in Greenland. This request was received at Ent Air Force Base in Colorado Springs for subsequent action by RCA Service Company, the current contractor.

An Air Force Colonel was assigned the task and he immediately contacted Dick as the RCA Contact. He already had a plan and was requesting Dick's assistance. Incidentally they had worked a couple of other projects in the past and had a very good working relationship. Essentially, they would travel to Greenland, visit all the sites in Greenland, create a preliminary document of JUNK, return to Colorado and finalize their plan. Needless to say this was a very big job.

The Colonel had the whole mission pretty much under control by the time Dick was able to get into Greenland. Dick flew directly to Thule, by way of McGuire AFB and Sondrestrom, where he met the Colonel to begin the initial survey. The Colonel had a helicopter with two pilots and a photographer on standby for their use anytime the weather was suitable for flying.

Thule was a very large base, having had a Wing of heavy bombers, a number of all-weather Interceptor Fighters, plus a rather large battery of Interceptor Missiles. Keep in mind when this Base was built it had the largest Radar Tracking station in the world, thus the extreme defenses.

Their first task was to identify, locate and photograph a number of the missile silos which needed to be removed since they were no longer operational. Apparently these missile silos required a tremendous amount of electricity since as Dick remembers there were three large (very large) wires that connected all of them to the power station. These wires, with insulation, were as large as a persons' leg. As a bit of trivia the original power station was a Power Ship, permanently moored in the harbor. Just another note of trivia; those missile silos were built of reinforced concrete and steel and they could not be destroyed with explosives, so what to do? Someone (probably a PHD, more likely a farmer) came up with a highly technical solution that worked wonders. Fill them with water, let them set through the winter and freeze and in the spring the concrete was completely shattered.

There were massive yards of excess construction equipment that needed to be identified and cataloged for removal, just to name a few collections of stuff that we reviewed. In addition, at the BMEWS site up on the hill where the main RADAR was located, there was much more STUFF that needed to be identified and cataloged.

After completing our identification, cataloging and photographing at Thule it was time to move our base of operation much further south down to Soderstrum Air Force Base. Soderstrum was much smaller than Thule, thus much less "stuff" that required cataloging; however there was at least one small satellite station that required our visitation. This site was a small LORAN navigational station that provided radio navigational aid to all types of aviation. We flew in one day with a plan to stay a couple of hours, and then return back to Soderstrum; however that plan quickly got changed due to weather. They came back with a chopper the next day to get us out. Trust me one day was plenty—feel sorry for those guys that stayed there for a couple of weeks at a time.

We had a couple of days in Soderstrum while waiting for a plane south so one of the more native Danish managers volunteered to take Dick for a hike to see what the rest of Greenland really looked like. This was a most interesting hike. They drove to the edge of the base and then travelled to the north out of Soderstrum towards a glacier, probably travelling some fifteen or more miles total. The time of the year was in the spring when the days were beginning to get longer and the bitter cold had broken.

Not too long after starting to hike they found a reindeer antler that had been shed the previous fall. Dick's new Danish friend told Dick that finding an antler like that was very uncommon as you generally had to buy them in the PX (store). Well low and behold after travelling another mile or so they found another, thus Dick now had a pair, free of charge. The next interesting event that they saw was a stampeding herd of reindeer on the opposite side of the valley. They sure did make lot of noise as they went by.

So what else could we possibly see next? Right out of the blue, probably about a two week old reindeer fawn walked right up to us like he really belonged there. Quite frankly Dick was very nervous, wondering where "Momma" was hiding; however we never did see Momma, in fact that fawn followed us for miles and almost back to the base.

Finally we got to see the glacier; however it was not too spectacular since we never got very close. Then low and behold we found a third antler, so Dick kept the best pair and brought them home. Getting them home took a bit of negotiating since Dick needed to take three different airlines to get back to Colorado Springs. Each time the stewardess just strapped them into an empty seat and with a bit of perseverance he got them home.

We were now in the final year of the contract so travel was beginning to slow down somewhat. During the early summer of 1975 Dick made his last trip to Alaska, visiting their buying facility in Anchorage, then on to the BMEWS site at Clear. In all his trips to Alaska he had never had a chance to visit Denali National Park so Dick made arrangements to go there on this trip. Several of the guys took a Day Trip bus ride out of Anchorage and visited the park.

Dick found it very interesting to learn the park service did not use any mechanical snow mobiles in patrolling the park. All such activities were accomplished by dog teams and sleds. NO SPARE PARTS, NO FUEL, NO BREAKDOWNS, etc. Seemed like a very logical move to him. Also the dogs provided much companionship, protection and warmth when needed. As a result of this trip Dick got very interested in Siberian Husky dogs and he ultimately acquired his first dog since losing King while he was stationed in Turkey many years ago in 1957. Getting a new dog resulted in many changes such as: learning to train and show dogs in Obedience, teaching obedience classes for many years and working with Service Dogs for the handicapped to name a few.

Before leaving Alaska, and particularly Clear, Dick must relate an interesting story that took place there. Precisely when this incident occurred has been lost in history but it brings back many fond memories. This incident occurred in the summer, when the sun was high in the sky at midnight. Sleeping on those nights was always a challenge and such was the case on this particular night. The time was probably around midnight when sleep was very elusive so Dick decided to take a walk, when he suddenly stumbled onto some horseshoe pits. Going back in time when Dick was stationed at Griffiss AFB he had become good friends with a much older Sergeant who believed Dick should learn to play horseshoes, thus the old Sergeant became Dick's mentor. His guidance and direction was, if you can't throw ringers you best get out of the game. Thus the old Sergeant spent much time in teaching Dick to Throw Ringers. Just as a passing note, Sarge had been stationed in Japan where he had become the NATIONAL Champion. Dick learned much from old Sarge. Now it is time to go back to Clear, Alaska.

Since Dick frequently had no competition, he learned to play one hand against the other and such was the case in Clear on that bright summer night, when a guy in a brand-new pick-um-truck pulled in and asked if Dick would be interested in a friendly little game of 'Shoes' since he had seen Dick playing by himself. He further stated he had his own 'custom shoes' in the truck and asked permission to use them which Dick gladly obliged. The stranger then made his big mistake. He stated that it would only be fair if he admitted that he had just recently been crowned Alaska State Champion. That flipped the switch and virtually everything Dick threw the rest of the night became a ringer. When the game was over Dick politely invited the stranger back for a rematch; however Dick had to leave before the stranger could return.

Before Dick leaves Colorado he must tell you about all of the many good times that he had while living in the west. First Dick will tell you about skiing. One of the first guys Dick hired out of the Air Force had worked in Cheyenne Mountain before coming to work at RCA, introduced Dick to downhill skiing. He was a temporary transplant from Ohio so he was not a lot better than Dick except he had spent several years there. They had a great time skiing Monarch for one day nearly every weekend that first winter. Needless to say Dick improved a great deal that winter, but then he had plenty of room for improvement.

Spring finally came and Dick's next door neighbor, a guy we will call Doc introduced him to back packing. Their first excursion was hiking to the top of Pikes Peak with a peak of 14,110 feet. They left Colorado Springs about noon, giving them plenty of time for a leisurely hike to the top. They spent the night just above timberline at close to 12,000 feet and that was the first time Dick ever witnessed the sun setting over that vast expanse of the Colorado prairie. Dick can see it like it was yesterday with two major highways providing two ribbons of light extending to the eastern horizon. As darkness progressed the ribbons just got brighter, then as it got later and traffic diminished the ribbons gradually faded away. Sunrise was just as spectacular in the morning. Fortunately, he got to see that sequence many times over the years since he eventually hiked Pikes Peak from every possible direction.

Over the years Doc and Dick took many extended hikes lasting for a week to ten days. Let me list just a few: Lost Creek Wilderness Area (4 day), Weminuche Wilderness Area (2 trips, each six days), Canyon Lands National Park, Utah (a group of six guys for ten days), Capitol Reef National Park, Utah (4 days), Bridger Wilderness Area, Utah (9 days), plus there were many more lasting for three to five days.

After the first year Doc and Dick began to do a lot more skiing and during the last couple of years they tried virtually all of the major ski areas in Colorado. Doc was a much better skier than Dick, thus Dick improved much under Doc's tutelage.

One of the winters while Dick was there, he and Doc decided to take a Wilderness Survival Course, conducted by the Outward Bound Organization since they were doing a lot of hiking in very wilderness areas and at relatively high altitudes, much above 12,000 feet. This organization was noted for taking delinquent or failing children and converting them into Rock Solid Citizens. They both came out of that course with a completely new understanding of Wilderness Survival. They studied building shelters, fishing without conventional equipment and making fires with NO conventional fire making equipment, in every kind of weather. They also had an intensive study on edible and non-edible plants and other things. For example, they learned which ants and other bugs are edible and how to prepare them for a feast. Dick must admit that removing the head from a large ant and plopping it in your mouth the first time can cause a bit of hesitation; however if you just think about starvation it becomes quite easy. Also, if your friends have just eaten their lunch it will almost always immediately cause them to lose their lunch.

During that last summer in Colorado Doc and Dick decided to take one last significant backpack trip into a wilderness area and the one they chose was the Weminuche Wilderness Area down near the southwestern corner of the state. They had been in there at least twice before; however these wilderness areas are so huge there is always more to see.

For those who have never hiked in wilderness areas, the experience is much different than hiking in a National Park or following a trail leading to the top of a mountain. First there are no trails, marked or otherwise. Generally there is a sign-in/sign-out register as you enter the area that contains your name and address and a point-of-contact if in the event your remains are located at some future date. Your expected date of return is completely unimportant since they will NEVER look for you.

Before going into a Wilderness Area it is important to have a good compass, good maps and a thorough understanding of how they both work. The other alternative is to have a highly keen sense of DEAD RECONING as was used by the pioneers.

Their plan for this trip was a stay of about ten days, with much of it at or above timberline with timberline generally being around 12,000 feet. They also generally anticipated covering an average of some fifteen to twenty miles per day. When starting a hike of this duration they usually started by carrying a pack weighing seventy to seventy-five pounds. Their normal gear included one two man tent, and a good sleeping bag and a ground matt for each man. Each man carried their own sleeping bag, ground cloth and their share of the food. Dick does not remember the reason, but he always carried the tent, probably due to the backpack configuration.

Doc was primarily the cook and Dick was in charge of setting up the tent and building a fire if one was needed. They almost always had a small camp fire and they kept it going until they called it a day. They, again almost always set up the tent due to sudden and unsuspected arrival of storms during the night. On about the third morning while Dick was cleaning up the area, Doc was reading the map when he suddenly realized they were a mere twenty miles or so from a place he had visited some three or four years before.

He told Dick that one of the pack companies had offered him a free pack trip in exchange for his services as being the company Doctor on that particular trip which he accepted.

Doc further went on to say they were only about twenty miles from one of the most spectacular camp sites he had ever seen. In an attempt to convince Dick that they should visit that site again, he tried to tell him all of the positive assets that this particular site had to offer. They included: located in a high mountain meadow with gorgeous scenery, plenty of water from a large flowing spring and plenty of fire wood for their evening fire. Before Dick states his decision, Dick must make a statement of fact. When hiking in a wilderness area with no specific destination, it really doesn't matter which way you go so he whole heartily endorsed the idea.

They pretty much hiked all day and arrived at the site at around three o'clock that afternoon. Before Dick tells you more, let Dick try to paint a picture in your mind of what he first saw. First, Dick must say the site was absolutely spectacular. Imagine a high mountain meadow stretching from horizon to horizon in every direction. You could probably see at least ten miles or more where ever you looked. They were just slightly above timberline and Dick estimates their elevation was at around 12,000 feet. Within this gorgeous landscape, single trees were scattered as far as the eye could see in every direction. These trees were some kind of pine with a maximum height of probably no more than twenty feet. Each of these trees were probably separated from each other by an estimated distance of at least 250 to 500 yards.

After Jack had given Dick the grand tour of the site; he showed Dick the spring with water bubbling out of the ground into a steady stream and last but not least he showed Dick a tree with the entire set of tent poles neatly stacked against it, awaiting the next pack train arrival.

The following conversation went something like so:

Doc: "Well Dick what do you think of the site?"

Dick: "Doc, the site is certainly everything you have said, it is most likely one of greatest campsites I have ever seen, but I will not be staying here tonight."

Doc: "What's the matter with you, are you nuts?"

The debate went on for a couple more exchanges with Doc becoming ever more confused when he finally said.

Doc: "What is it precisely that you don't like?'

Dick: "Doc is there anything about all of these trees that strikes you as very odd?

Doc: "Well not really except every tree over ten to fifteen feet tall are all dead."

Dick: "But why are they all dead?"

Doc: "I have no clue, do you know why?"

Dick: "Doc every tree as far as you can see in every direction has been struck by lightning. That is the reason this site has so much fire wood for camp fires. Look carefully and you will quickly see the trees are completely dead from fire and the vast majority of the trunks are completely shattered from top to bottom. These are all classic symptoms of lightning damage".

Doc then told Dick a story about his previous trip to this site some three years prior. Apparently they arrived midafternoon, got their tent set up just in time to have shelter from a severe storm and then waited for the storm to clear.

After the storm had passed, they went out of their tent to survey the area for damage and they discovered one of their pack horses had been struck by lightning and lay belly up in their camp site. The horse had some additional damage—both front legs were missing from the elbow down.

After Doc understood why Dick would not stay there that night, he was very happy to find a new place to bed down. They left this gorgeous site and dropped down into the heavy woods below timberline and found reasonable shelter there. There is still just a little more to this story.

That night they encountered the severest thunderstorm of all of their backpacking adventures, in fact that night is the only night they ever got wet and they ended up with a full tent of water. It took the entire next day to get their equipment dry enough to press on.

Back on the job with RCA, the end of a contract typically carries with it a few very difficult tasks that must be done; however this time there was one situation that exemplifies why ex-military employees are different, and the story must be told. First, very near the end of a contract every manager must advise each and every faithful employee that their services are no longer needed. This task usually occurs about two weeks prior to termination of the contract and such was the case with this contract. Even though all the critical people are no longer working, all of those critical tasks are expected to continue to be accomplished. Such was the case on this contract.

With about a week to go, the Air Force contacted Dick and indicated there was a severe FUELS problem up on the Line that needed immediate attention. Dick had absolutely no idea where to begin as all of his fuels experts had been laid off. The question quickly became, so what to do now?

Dick's two fuels experts had heard about the problem through their connections and called Dick to offer their services. Dick advised them they could not do that since they were no longer on the payroll. They even offered to come in without pay. Again Dick had to refuse their offer.

The following morning the Air Force called to advise Dick the problem had been resolved and thus there was no longer a problem. When Dick quarried the two fuels guys he got very little information; however, somehow they convinced the guard to allow them entry into a secure place, they resolved the problem and no one will ever know how they did it since they are both gone. This is just one more example of why working with the military/ex-military has always been such a pleasure, no such a privilege.

This is also the perfect place for Dick to pass on a bit of information regarding employees. My praise for ex-military employees has been frequent and profound; however, it must be said again. Dick having worked for four major corporations over a forty year span, ex-military employees, whether retired or just individuals who have previously severed their country, their understanding of commitment and dedication far exceed that of any other group of employees. It was a pleasure, no it was an HONOR, to have had the privilege of working with them.

The end of the BMEWS/DEW Line contract was quickly coming to a close so it was time to begin thinking about the future. RCA had offered Dick a job in managing one of their subsidiary companies, AlaskaCom in Anchorage, Alaska; however having been travelling there for the past several years he was fully aware of the extremely high cost of living, plus he would be moving in the wrong direction. Therefore after many great years and many super opportunities with RCA, Dick and Joy decided to move back east to the upstate New York area. There were many more job opportunities in New York versus Colorado, plus Dick's mother was in very poor health; therefore it was not a difficult decision. Since Dick was leaving RCA it was time to thank them for all of the opportunities they had given him.

They gave him opportunities that very few people can only dream about and he hopes he has given you a glimpse of some of his many adventures. However, once settled in New York there were still many new opportunities that were just awaiting their discovery.

Before moving on Dick must also take a few minutes to talk about many of the people he met, became acquainted with and yes, in many cases became lifelong friends. Generally speaking RCA was much more military oriented than any other company that he was ever associated with. Starting at Griffiss AFB, once outside of the data processing world nearly all of his acquaintances were either in the military, or had had extensive military experience and exposure. That was not true with any other groups of people he worked with.

Dick takes time to mention this military connection for a very specific reason. Based on his experiences, this military training gave them a significant advantage over the organizations that had little or no military background or association since individuals with a military background/training KNOW HOW TO GET THINGS DONE. They have been trained for life, NOT the next test.

Unfortunately, many of my very close friends have passed on to their final rewards, but I continue to keep in touch with the few that are left.

Chapter Six

AFTER RCA

In 1975 Dick's association with RCA came to a close and it was time to move on. The decision had been made to move back to New York as previously stated however there were several events that occurred in the business communities that would have a direct impact on his future career.

In the fall of 1975 Dick accepted a position working for Agway Inc. in their Corporate Headquarters, which was located on the southeastern side of Syracuse, New York. This position was a classic Systems Architect job and the specific task was to identify, define and build a new logistics system that could be installed in each of their three regionally located warehouses. These were located in Geneva, New York, a second located in Harrisburg, Pennsylvania and a third located in Springfield, Massachusetts. Each warehouse served all retail stores within their region.

The overall plan was to allow associated stores to have direct access to all warehouse information that included product availability, pricing and direct ordering capability. In addition, each warehouse would have its own computer hardware and software. This was a pretty tall order; however certainly within Dick's capability. As you may remember he had built a much larger system for NASA that supported over a hundred Apollo radar tracking stations around the world. Dick's initial task then was to develop a plan to satisfy these requirements, complete with cost estimates to cover system development, implementation and hardware. This was a long time ago but the initial estimate was well over a half million dollars to cover necessary equipment, programming and training, etc.

Dick submitted his analysis on hard copy (vary smart move) that detailed each cost, including hardware, programming and implementation. The boss nearly had a heart attack. Apparently he had never seen a study anything like that before, instead all previous estimates had just been verbal, thus easily subject to change as required. The boss did make an interesting comment that was duly noted and that was, "This estimate is far above anything the company is willing to spend at this time so we will give the BOSS (President of the company) an estimate of $75,000 and then after the project is well under way we will go back and explain we had made a mistake in our original analysis but we have much invested and they will give us the necessary funding to continue.

In conjunction with accepting a position of working for Agway, Dick and Joy still owned their home in Colorado Springs, Colorado that they needed to sell, plus they needed to find and purchase a new home that was located in the Utica/Clinton area in New York. In order to get all of these critical tasks completed in the least possible time, Joy went back to Colorado to sell the house and take care of arranging the move back to New York. During that same time frame Dick needed to locate a suitable house that they could afford and make the necessary arrangements to purchase that house.

The house that Dick found was in an ideal location; however the house itself was a real fixer-upper. The house had been lived in by a very old couple for many years and thus needed a thorough bath, both inside and out before Joy arrived with all the furniture. All of those tasks were completed just in time. Incidentally, Joy was devastated when she got her first look at their 'new' house but that went away quickly once they started to move in. Actually the house is well over two hundred years old and thus has much history associated with it. It is situated on the old Seneca Turnpike and was directly across the road from the old Lairdsville Inn, the largest inn between Utica and Syracuse at that time. Another bit of trivia, General George Washington owned a farm less than two miles away and thus spent a lot of time at the Lairdsville Inn.

The time of year was the first week of December but there was still no snow on the ground which was very fortunate since their large Siberian Husky dog needed a place to run. They had just enough time to get the yard built before heavy snow arrived.

If you remember earlier, the first job that Dick had after leaving the Air Force was a maintenance type job at an Oneida County Hospital. Well, this is the first chance when all of that experience really paid big dividends.

When the house was purchased it was known that the electrical wiring was in very bad condition. Therefore due to time constraints Dick hired an electrical contractor to install a new electric service entrance so he could begin completely rewiring the house and bringing it up to current standards. That task took virtually all of Dick's spare time throughout the remainder of the winter.

During that same winter they had decided they needed a barn for storage, therefore the following summer they decided to build a new barn. This barn would be thirty-two feet long by twenty- eight feet wide with a single large door on the front. The barn would also have a gambrel roof with six sky lights in the roof, thus giving it a full second floor. Dick's new friend and neighbor would help him with all of the heavy lifting, particularly building and setting the rafters. Again Dick's experience that he gained at the hospital was invaluable.

Getting back to Agway; their project to develop a monstrous on-line customer ordering system for their warehouses apparently had run into the expected funding problems. In keeping with past traditions Dick had noticed at least two employees had suddenly disappeared and he was now convinced he would be next. Dick had concluded that 'firing a person or two' was the normal way of getting management off the hook for any and all of their bad decisions, as in fact the position that Dick had filled had been vacated for that very same reason. It was for that reason that EVERY CONVERSATION he had with everyone was carefully documented and retained as he quickly saw the next lamb on its way to the slaughter house.

During this time Dick developed a very good working relationship with two or three of the Agway Directors. This was a very good move. Before the final meeting he made sure each of the Directors had a complete package of all documentation that he had accumulated. On Friday shortly after lunch, a group of several individuals were invited to the office of the Agway President. This group included the Systems Manager, the Computer Department Manager, several tag a longs (witnesses he suspected) plus Dick. The Systems Manager opened the meeting by explaining how badly Dick had miscalculated and miss represented the cost of building and implementing the proposed warehouse computer equipment and associated software. Little did he know that EVERYBODY that was ANYBODY had a copy of the original cost analysis in their possession.

Dick had fully expected that when the time came that the BOSS was made fully aware of the actual cost for developing that very grandiose system, the corporation would withdraw all funding and cancel the entire project. That time had just arrived. As you will notice, again an employee's job would need to be sacrificed in order to save the jobs' of management. During a lengthy discussion with the President, all funding for the project was withdrawn and in the meantime the lesser managers all snuck out of the door, never to be seen or heard from again.

Since Dick had certainly been expecting to be leaving Agway sometime in the reasonably near future, he had been preparing for that eventuality. Therefore, using some of the many skills he had acquired along the way he began doing subcontracting work to fill the gap in pay. Another large plus was the fact that Dick no longer was required to drive 120 miles each day to Syracuse.

Again "*DESTINY*" took control. Dick did in fact get *FIRED* as expected however it was only a couple of months before Agway unexpectedly closed and locked their doors, never to be reopened, therefore he would have lost his job anyway. By getting fired he was ahead of all the others in looking for a new job. While on the subject of layoffs and getting fired Dick must make a comment. Many times you get comfortable with a job and because of familiarity you just hang on as was his case with Agway. Getting fired was just what was needed to relight the fire as you will see. Nearly always you end up better after the event than if the event had never happened. For example, Dick had been laid off twice before and each time he dramatically improved his situation, as was the case this time.

There was much activity occurring in the business world that Dick had previously been living in for the past decade or more and the first major consolidation took place when General Electric purchased RCA (Radio Corporation of America). Apparently NBC (National Broadcasting Company) was the primary plumb that GE was after since there were a number of other smaller subsidiary companies that were simply sold. These included; Random House Books, Hertz Rent a Car, and Cornet Industries, to name a few.

It must have been *"DESTINY"* that appeared again. Let me try to explain. First, GE had a very strong presence in New York and the northeast with major plants in Utica, Syracuse, Binghamton, Schenectady, and Burlington, Vermont, and at about the same time they were also looking for someone with extensive experience in large computer systems design and implementation of projects. This particular job was located in Utica and was much closer than the previous 50/60 mile drive to Syracuse plus the recent acquisition of RCA by GE provided the possibility of potentially reinstating RCA pension credits.

The new job that Dick ultimately accepted was with General Electric, located in Utica, New York, less than ten miles from home. GE had just created a new organization that would be specializing in the development of what they termed Common Systems with Dick being the Lead Systems Architect in that organization. So what is a Common System? A Common System is a system that is uniquely designed to have the ability to support more than one business, based on varying parameters. This relationship resulted in the perfect fit for Dick in both the short and long term as you will see.

On Dick's very first day at work, Dick's new Manager took him to the Broad Street plant where all of Utica Finance was located, including the Credit and Collections organization, managed by a fellow that Dick will refer to as Jack. The meeting was attended by Dick and his Manager from the computer department, and Jack and his number one assistant. For some unknown reason (unknown at that time) Dick and his boss were met with a great deal of animosity which struck Dick as very odd since they were there to help, or so they thought. However there was much bad blood between Dick's boss and Jack which Dick was obviously not aware of. Dick suggested they postpone the meeting for a couple of days to allow the room temperature to return to normal.

The first thing the following morning Dick called Jack and requested that just the two of them sit down and have a good old fashioned heart to heart talk and yes, Jack's number one assistant was also invited. The meeting was scheduled for right after lunch that day.

The meeting began on a very sour note when the assistant walked into the room and the very first thing he said was, "Well what kind of shit are you going to ram down our throats this time?" Dick's immediate response was, "Let me ask you a question. When you go out to a restaurant for dinner, does the waitress tell you what you are going to eat?" His response was, "Well No". Dick responded, "Well I'm not going to tell you what you are going to eat either". Before we go any further Dick said he believed it would be appropriate for him to give you (Jack) a bit of information about Dick's history.

In 1958 Dick received his discharge from the Air Force with the rank of Staff Sergeant after serving four years as a Meteorologist. In 1960 Dick was hired by RCA as a trainee in their computer department on the night shift with absolutely no experience and/or college education. So why did they hire him? He has never been able to answer that question. In any case with hard work he received a promotion to Night Shift Supervisor with approximately ten people working for him. Dick always suspected the reason for that promotion was his military training. This promotion at RCA took place after approximately only four to five months on the job.

Within the first year Dick had learned how to program the IBM 650 computer and was very soon doing much of their programming. Programming was very straight forward; however designing computer systems was a completely different situation. Even those individuals with college degrees had a great deal of difficulty in providing the customer with a product they could or would use as Dick had just experienced.

So Dick said to Jack, "Probably your next question should be why I believe this system would be different than all the others".

When Dick began designing systems he discovered the same hard cold facts of life that virtually all system designers discover, and experienced the same frustrations of failure. Many designers turn to academia for the answers however that is not where the answers are located. Persistence and hard work will occasionally reveal the avenue to success, assuming you can withstand the many frustrations along the way.

After numerous trials and many errors Dick discovered the *secret*. The answer is always right in front of you in the form of the requester and ultimate user of the new system. Just spend a lot of time with the customer, and using the correct techniques to determine what they really want/need versus trying to ram something you have learned in a college text book down their throat and you will be a winner *EVERY* time. Dick has built Payroll, Accounting, Engineering, Inventory Control, and Banking systems plus many others—all very successfully. He has built large systems for the Air Force (supporting BMEWS and the DEW Line in the Arctic), the Navy in the Bahamas (supporting AUTEC-Atlantic Underwater Test and Evaluation Center), and NASA (specifically supporting the APPOLO Radar Tracking Stations around the world of which there were nearly one hundred).

The very first step is to always complete the broad outline of the system requirements, as defined by the ultimate user, then identify preliminary reports and insure that all requirements are feasible. Once that is complete it is possible to develop rough cost and development time estimates etc.

Then it is time to go back and begin to fill in all of the missing details such as report layouts, file structures, begin defining the many data elements, plus defining a plan for organization structure. You must also develop simulated reports for all major activities and users. By this time you will understand the new system well enough to speak intelligently to any interested individuals.

Therefore, the time had now come to begin including other associates and higher level management to obtain their recommendations, suggestions and buy-in into the plan. The first such meeting included Jack's manager, the Utica Department Manager of Finance and much of his staff. Essentially this meeting became just a formality as there was no discussion or recommendations. Dick believed they had never attended a meeting such as that, one that required some thought and participation. The Utica Manager of Finance approved the document as written without ever even reading it.

A few days later they had a similar meeting with the Division Manager of Finance (DMF) and his entire staff. This guy was very small in stature, with a reputation more in accordance with a six foot, two hundred fifty pound linebacker. Thus Dick's new boss and his boss's boss, the Manager of the entire Computer Operation decided they should accompany Dick to the meeting and at least give him moral support. Apparently they didn't know that for the past ten years that this was the world that Dick had been living in. In any case the meeting was completely between the Division Manager of Finance and Dick. Several times he asked questions that Dick had no idea what he was talking about. In each case Dick gave him the same answer that he did not know but would get the answer and get back to him in a day or so. As you will see, Dick made a very close friend that day, in a very high place that served him very, very well for many years to come.

When the meeting broke up, Dick's new manager, and Dicks' manager's boss (the Computer Center Manager) left quickly and was quite some distance ahead of Jack and Dick when suddenly the DMF shouted in a voice that everyone in that part of the building could hear, "Dick, the next time you come to my office you leave those other two ass holes home". Dick went to see the DMF many times after that but almost always alone.

Since they had sold the proposed system (to the user and all of top management) it was now time to deliver the goods and this is the way that was done.

Before Dick describes the way the system was built he must first describe the difference in the utilization of personnel between RCA and now General Electric. In RCA they had a category of people that were referred to as Systems Analysts whose function was to both design the proposed system and then perform the physical programming, or in other words writing the machine code.

In General Electric they had Systems Architects and Computer Programmers. In this structure the Architects designed the entire system and the Programmers wrote the code that was necessary to accomplish the task(s). Since this was Dick's first system at General Electric he immediately switched to the new structure and quickly found it much better than the older system he had always used previously.

It was now time for Dick to start building his first system in GE using their personnel structure. Dick would do all of the system/ program design work and associated documentation, then turn the system documentation over to the Programmer for computer coding and development where the Programmer is the expert in software development.

For the remainder of his career, Dick would always function as the Systems Architect, then work very closely with the highly technical computer programmers for system implementation.

The Programmer lives in the technical world and as such must constantly be upgrading their skills just to stay even with the rapidly changing technology in both the hardware and software worlds. In fact the changes may come so fast it is impossible to keep up with all of them. Therefore the Programmer must be highly skilled in all aspects of program development and hardware interface.

On the other hand the Systems Architect must have very strong interpersonal skills since they will be working very closely with everyone from clerks to very high level management. They must be able to tease the minutest details from all those in between. Once they have acquired the details they must then be able to convert all that information into a format that will allow the Programmer to build the necessary program code.

Since Dick was new at GE it was now time to identify the people that he would be working with and get them on his team. After starting work at GE he noticed a couple of significant differences between the two companies. As he has previously noted RCA had a much higher percentage of ex-military type personnel than did GE, thus the higher military component directly impacted the work ethic as well as the dress code.

One of the first major differences Dick noticed between RCA and GE was the dress code. At RCA if you were working you would always be dressed appropriately for the job at hand, for example a dress shirt and tie for all management and associated personnel. Their dress code was very similar to what you would find in the military. They had a favorite saying; "Just Remember, You Never Get A Second Chance To Make Another First Impression". At GE it appeared that the more sloppily you looked the better dressed you were considered to be. One day at coffee break Dick walked into the break room, dressed in white shirt and tie, slacks and sport coat and a manager/want-to be shouted across the room and asked if he was having an interview today and Dick's simple reply; "Well, no as a matter of fact, I am not digging a ditch today, and I am not shoveling shit today and no, I am not even having an interview today so it must be somewhere in between". That ended all future discussions.

Now back to Dick locating his first Programmer. Dick went to management and requested a young Programmer that Dick will refer to as John. Why did Dick want John? John just didn't seem to fit into the pattern of all the others that were available and, he was not interested in being a social butterfly as were many others. John also had a couple of characteristics or qualities the others lacked. Number one, he was ex-military, having spent two years in the Army completing his ROTC obligation, then getting out of the Army holding the Rank of Second Lieutenant. With this background he knew the meaning of obligation and leadership.

As Dick told management he wanted someone to work *WITH* him, not for him. Dick's choice resulted in him selecting the best Programmer that he ever worked with and he remained with Dick for many years until Dick retired. In fact, until Dick met John, Dick truly believed he was the best programmer ever born. John made him eat some humble pie.

Since Dick could not even spell Credit and Collections he decided getting a good name would be someplace appropriate to start. Following is then a detailed list of all the steps Dick would follow in developing the new Credit and Collections system as told to the Manager of that organization.

1) First they would begin by developing a Master List of all the major components and functions that YOU (the customer) want your new system to address. The customer, in this case had never heard of that idea before.

2) Next, after this broad list is complete, the designer will go back and review each item on the Master List and begin adding details to include reports, data elements, formulas, etc.

3) The designer will identify every report and/or online inquiry that the user will require to access and maintain their information. The designer will further ensure the capability exists to both input and or maintain every data element within the data base.

4) The designer will now insure the system either contains *every* data element that you, the user will need, or the system will have the ability to compute that information.

5) After the designer has gathered all the requirements and data elements, based on the user inputs, the designer will prepare a simulation of each report, inquiry and/or update that you, the user will require.

6) After your complete and thorough review (and any corrections have been made) you, the user will sign and date that document and that will become the measure that will be used to determine the adequacy of the system. Any and all changes will be thoroughly documented.

7) Everything had now been approved and the real work began. It was now time for the designer to communicate with the programmer(s) and define EVERY I/O function, every option, every decision, etc. This task is accomplished by preparing detailed program specifications, to include all data elements, every decision the program must make, etc. for the programmer.

John and Dick quickly became a very close working team and the Manager of Credit and Collections was almost immediately able to see his new system taking shape, and believe it or not it was exactly what he had wanted months earlier.

Based on many past experiences and by following the methodology outlined above, the Credit and Collections system did in fact become operational AND DID MEET all expectations as promised.

Not long after the system became operational Dick received a call from his new friend, the Division Manager of Finance who was asking for a comprehensive slide presentation to be prepared for his boss, the Division General Manager who was located in Valley Forge. Dick put together a very detailed presentation that took about two hours to give and then the Division Manager of Finance reviewed it in great detail with Dick, making a few minor changes, then the Division Manager of Finance sent the Utica Manager of Credit and Collections and Dick off to Valley Forge. Little did they know what lay in store for them the next day.

The next day when they arrived in Valley Forge they were taken directly into the inner office of the Division General Manager where he stated that the next day's meeting would be with the *Corporate* Manager of Finance, and we would be presenting our new system to him and his staff. He next stated that this was his meeting and wanted to know if we would prefer to present in the morning or afternoon. Dick thought Jack, the Manager of Credit and Collections was going to have a heart attack based on the quickness of Dick's answer stating we wanted to be first in the morning. The Division General Manager further wanted to know why it was important for us to be first. Dick's reply was simply, "After my two hour detailed presentation, followed by Jack's hour long live demonstration there will be no questions left to ask". Thus it was so.

After lunch Corporate gave their presentation which was quite simply a reading of the objectives for a system they were planning to build sometime in the future. As suspected virtually every objective for their proposed system was already included in the system that had just been presented, and demonstrated in the morning. The afternoon session was remarkably short.

As originally predicted in the very first meeting between Dick and Jack, the Manager of Credit and Collections, his system could, and then did become, the first corporate wide system ever developed. Not only that, it was done in Utica where no other common system had ever been developed.

NOTE: Jack became the King of Credit and Collections corporate wide.

Having left Colorado the previous summer and having gotten settled into his new home it was now time to explore new areas for adventure. It was not long before an opportunity presented itself. Downhill skiing was available but downhill skiing in New York is a lot different than skiing where Dick had learned to ski in Colorado, one of the skiing capitols of the world.

In the spring Dick had become acquainted with a group of about twenty people who had done quite a bit of white water rafting, and more specifically on the Cheat River in northwestern West Virginia south of Pittsburg, Pa. The Cheat River in the spring when the river is high was considered to have some of the best white water in the east.

Their plan was to take a day of vacation on Friday and travel to Morgantown, West Virginia where they would spend the night at a camp ground, then 'shoot' the river on Saturday. On Saturday morning they took a bus to the river where they acquired wet suits, life jackets and instructions.

Basically they used two sizes of rafts for the run. The most common raft held six people while the smaller raft held only four. Incidentally they duplicated that same adventure two years in a row and on both occasions Dick was lucky enough to take the trip in the smaller raft. The small raft was much faster, with significantly less horse power to maneuver (two less bodies to provide power to steer) and much greater opportunity for getting thrown out of the raft. If in fact you were thrown overboard you were unable to get back in the raft until you came out of the rapids and reached smoother water downstream. On Saturday after the raft trip they had a big steak cookout, followed by a most welcome night of sleep on the lean-to floor. Sunday was reserved for the return trip home.

As previously stated that during one of Dick's many trips to Alaska he had become acquainted with the Husky breed of dogs while visiting Denali National Park. While they were still living in Colorado they had located a breeder of those dogs and had acquired a Black and White bitch that they named Tanya. Dick was determined this time to learn more about dog obedience than he had known when he was just a kid, training his old friend King, thus Dick located a woman in Colorado Springs that had a very good reputation for teaching dog obedience and signed up for a few lessons. Training was progressing nicely when it was time to move back to New York.

As quickly as possible Dick located another highly regarded dog trainer, located in Clinton, New York whom Dick will refer to as Sandy. This meeting resulted in them having a very long working relationship. Sandy convinced Dick he should consider showing Tanya in Obedience Competition so he commenced working toward that goal.

Dick had never had a goal for competition but he guesses it was just supposed to occur, "DESTINY". He knew nothing about obedience competition; in fact he had never even seen an obedience trial. Therefore, one Saturday morning it was time to load Tanya into the car and find out what competition was all about. They arrived at the trial and Dick fortunately met an elderly lady who agreed to coach him a bit about the procedures. She said, "You just do what I do".

Apparently her guidance was good since by the end of the day Tanya had taken "Best of Show". Needless to say Dick was hooked on another sport and ultimately trained/showed many dogs over the next thirty years. Sandy was also duly impressed and immediately offered Dick a job teaching obedience classes for her. Dick taught for her for many years in the Clinton Arena. Sandy was also very good to him since she always gave him all the big and ugly dogs which proved to be a major advantage.

Many years earlier when living in Remsen Dick had become friends with a local veterinarian who had taken care of his many pets which included dogs, cats, two horses and chickens. Some ten or twelve years later when they returned to the Utica area they renewed their friendship and got their animals back up to snuff. During one of those visits Dick's friend the veterinarian indicated he was in the market for a reliable crew member on his sail boat as he was an avid sailor. Having never even been on a sail boat it sounded like something Dick really should try. After the first encounter Dick was hooked for many years.

They sailed (raced) nearly every Wednesday night, and sometimes on Saturday and Sunday, on Oneida Lake where Dick's friend moored his boat. Each race had at least three legs, essentially forcing everyone to sail into all points of the wind. A typical race would consist of two fleets, the first fleet was comprised of all those boats that had won a race during the current racing season, and the second fleet contained all other non-winners. Dick's friend was an outstanding sailor and teacher so they rarely ever sailed in the second fleet. His friend also had a pretty much middle of the road yacht being twenty four feet in length and made by Able Fuchsine (spelling). They almost always flew the spinnaker on at least one leg of the race. It was a rare day that they did not finish in the money and there were many first and second place finishes in the trophy case. Incidentally, Dick has never sailed in a sail boat that was not in a race.

It is time now to tell a racing story. Two or three years had passed and Dick's friend, whom we will call Skipper decided to join in a partnership with a friend of his and invest in a significantly larger boat. This boat was nearly a thirty foot vessel; however the make has been lost to the ages. In any case the smaller boat could be raced by just the Skipper and Dick; however, the new boat required a crew of at least three. Regardless, they purchased the boat late in the racing season and took delivery just in time to participate in the Labor Day Regatta. During the racing season all boats were divided into two fleets. The first fleet contained all the boats that had won a race during the racing season and the second fleet contained all of the rest. Obviously, Skippers boat would be racing in the second fleet since he had never even sailed it yet.

The Regatta consisted of four races on; Friday night, Saturday, Sunday and Monday. Keep in mind they took delivery of the new boat, during the day on Friday, just in time to enter the First Race on Friday evening. Skipper ended up winning that race, much to the chagrin of all of the other contestants; however, Saturday was a new day, a new race course and still a new boat.

Low and behold, on the second leg of the race the wind completely stopped blowing and everyone became becalmed. To many racers a break in the wind was an indicator that it was time for a beer, but not for Skipper. By paying strict attention to details Skipper kept his boat on course and just barely moving in the water. After about an hour the wind picked up to near gale force of maybe one knot (possibly two miles per hour). By using what little breeze there was, Skipper had kept his boat on course and just barely moving. Finally the wind picked up a bit more and everyone got back to Sailing; however, since everyone forgot about sailing and thought more about drinking a beer, their boats were in complete disarray, with none moving and many headed 180 degrees off course. Incidentally, turning a boat around and getting restarted once you are completely stopped is a very difficult task, thus the reason for keeping the boat moving if at all possible. Again, skill rears its ugly head.

Since Skipper's boat was headed in the proper direction and still moving (although very slowly) they were off like a shot. Long story short, not only did they win the race, but they also beat everyone else on the lake. They were accused of starting their engine and many other kinds of cheating, when in reality it was simply good boats man ship. Skipper now had two wins in the Regatta, needing only one more to win the Regatta, with two more races to go.

After the big win on Saturday, the powers to be placed Skipper and his boat in the first fleet for the third race on Sunday. There were no unusual events that day other than they won. It took three wins to win the Regatta so Skipper passed racing on Monday.

By the early 1980's Dick and his selection of John as his senior programmer had established a very strong reputation for building Common Systems. Common Systems were generally defined as a system that could be implemented by multiple businesses, in multiple locations. In fact, Dick and John were the only team that ever built a successful Common System any place within GE/Lockheed Martin that this writer is aware of. They built several smaller common systems, such as Payroll, and then they built the CORT System, the largest computer system ever built completely within Lockheed/ Martin Corporation. The CORT System is discussed in much greater detail in a chapter by itself.

The Payroll system that they upgraded was a Payroll system that after completion became the second common System that was used throughout their division. Basically they converted an old system from the antiquated old technology of magnetic tape (sequential processing) into a much more modern and sophisticated direct access technology system using the significantly more powerful IDMS software. The Payroll system gave them all a great deal of experience with the new software that would be used on virtually all future systems.

While John was the key person on the Payroll system there was much activity elsewhere. As the old saying goes, with a couple of major successes behind them, the more requests they would get for their services, and so it was. In fact they got so many requests that they were authorized to hire two new people. After much searching Dick chose to hire two young men fresh out of college. The first thing John and Dick had to do was to remove all the college mentality about building computer systems. John had the responsibility of making them great programmers and Dick's responsibility was to acquaint them to a whole new systems development philosophy. John and Dick were both very successful as they ended up with two great employees.

While all of the above activities were taking place Jack, Manager of Credit and Collections had developed some ideas about his new Credit and Collections system that could and would significantly improve cash flow, thus he and Dick began a week-long trip to propose and coordinate those ideas with the affected organizations. GE had a young guy that travelled to Boston for a couple of days each week to facilitate the movement of paper through the government system. For the sake of this discussion we will refer to this young fellow as Joe. Joe had developed several important contacts at the Defense Finance and Accounting Services Office (DFAS) in Boston. Those contacts proved very useful as they helped develop system improvements that would enhance the flow of government payments directly to the bank of GE's choice. Their next stop in Boston was at the Shawmut Bank where virtually all of GE banking from DFAS took place.

Did the effort in Boston have any impact? You be the judge. Processing times from DFAS payments fell from nearly thirty days to usually overnight. Just consider the magnitude of the impact when hundreds of payments (worth millions of dollars) were thusly affected. The next stop on this trip was to GE's processing bank in New York City (name forgotten), then to Kansas City to the Boatman's bank. Incidentally, while passing through Kansas City Jack and Dick had enough time to visit the Gateway ARCH in St. Louis between flights. From there they went on to GE's other Banks in Dallas, then on to San Francisco. All in all this was a most productive trip.

Sometime during the early eighties Dick finally obtained his Private Pilot's License. Shortly after getting His license he had an opportunity to purchase a Piper Cherokee PA-28 180 which he kept for nearly twenty years. He was forced to sell it during his seventies due to the extremely high cost of insurance, retirement and other very high maintenance costs.

Throughout much of that time he was also a member of the Utica/Rome Squadron of the Civil Air Patrol. Although he was both qualified and certified to fly their planes (generally Cessna 172 and 182) he preferred to fly as the Observer. With a great deal of photography experience he was soon flying virtually all of their photography missions. There were three missions that remain vivid memories; however the years are getting a bit fuzzy. The first of those missions involved a major snow and ice storm covering the area essentially west of Utica to Buffalo and north to the St Lawrence River. The storm took down literally hundreds of miles of power and telephone lines, most roads were closed, farmers could not milk their cows, and many could not even feed their cattle.

The aircraft they were flying on that mission had equipment that they could take photographs and transmit the photo directly to Mission Operations in Albany. Albany could and did give the air crew coordinates for specific areas of concern.

The second major mission that Dick photographed was for a documentary of the New York City watershed. They photographed all the applicable lakes, rivers, aqueducts and tunnels; using maps that identified everything that needed to be photographed.

The third major mission was to photograph a simulated terrorist attack on a tour boat in the Chesapeake Bay. Incidentally, while flying that specific mission, that is the only time that Dick ever got air sick.

That mission required that Dick (the photographer) fly in the back seat, while operating the camera in very rough air, all the while looking through the camera view finder. It still turned out to be a success.

Dick told you earlier that the house he had purchased when they moved back from Colorado to New York was a real fixer-upper. Well that was true. This time a large porch on the front of the house needed some major attention. It was decided that they should remove the entire structure and replace it with an up-to-date sun space. Thus in the mid 1970's it was time to start. Since there was going to be a small amount of government energy rebates involved, they needed architectural drawings, therefore it was time to seek the services of another very good friend, who just happened to be an architect and a teacher at MVCC (Mohawk Valley Community College).

The design called for a sun space that was approximately twelve feet wide and approximately twenty-four feet long. The front of the porch, or south facing side would have five windows that were approximately four feet wide and six feet high. The southerly facing roof exposure would have the exact same window configuration. In the summer a ninety percent sun screen is used to reduce the heat input; however in the winter when the sun screen is removed the porch will produce enough heat to heat the entire house whenever the sun is shining. Also whenever the sun is shining and there is excess heat available, a large imbedded ceiling fan automatically turns on to move that excess heat throughout the entire house, thus suspending operation of the normal heating system.

In the winter and spring of 1991 Dick found out that this same friend was going to be teaching a special course at MVCC tailored especially for contractors that would teach them all about the budding new technology of geothermal heating and cooling. This course would give Dick a chance to get in on the ground floor of this exciting new technology. Well guess what, Dick took a week's vacation from GE and took that course.

As soon as Dick finished the course, he began the design of his own geo-thermal heat pump system, with installation beginning as soon as the ground could be broken in the spring. For all you technocrats the following is a very brief description of the system;

Heat pump Unit—Five Ton

Pipe in the ground -- 2000 feet of one inch plastic pipe

Four independently controlled Fan Coil heat exchangers for distribution of heat/air conditioning throughout the house.

As of this writing the system has only been operational for approximately twenty-five years, therefore we are still in the TESTING phase of this installation. Incidentally the system also provides nice refreshing air-conditioning on those hot summer nights. This installation also became one of the first geothermal systems to be installed in upstate New York.

On a more personal note in 1991 Dick's wife Joy Ann was diagnosed with cancer of the liver. I cannot remember how many surgeries, radiation treatments, and hospitalizations she had throughout the following two year period. Finally in September 1993 she passed away after being married for thirty-six years. For those who have experienced the loss of your life long partner you will understand. Thank God for the companionship of my dogs.

Later in 1994 Dick's very close Veterinary friend introduced him to a long time employee of his whom Dick will refer to as Mary who had much experience as a Veterinary Technician. She also had much experience with animals of all kinds but particularly cats and dogs. Mary, along with her family had also done significant amounts of travelling and camping so she and Dick had much in common. Mary convinced Dick that they should spend a weekend at Letchworth State Park and try camping her way versus backpacking for miles through some wilderness area in the Rocky Mountains. Thus it was so. They didn't have a lot of gear but still had a great time.

As a result of their Letchworth experience they purchased a medium sized Fifth Wheel camper that they towed with Dick's truck and that was the beginning of literally thousands of miles of travel throughout North America. Many of those travels are detailed elsewhere in this book. Incidentally, Dick and Mary have added nearly one hundred thousand miles of travel over the years to that truck, using three different configurations of camping equipment. The vast majority of that travel included two, sometimes three large dogs. The areas visited while travelling included nearly all of the continental United States and much of Canada.

Chapter Seven

CORT COUNCIL

In the Spring of 1984 Dick received another assignment to build another new system. The original assignment was to build a Shipment Billing system as a Common System; however, after much serious research and consultation with the accountants Dick concluded that building a new system by starting in the middle would be a disaster. He even gave serious consideration to building a Shipping System, since virtually all of the information that would be needed to build a Shipment Billing System would be needed in a Shipping System.

The more Dick researched and consulted with all the parties involved, he finally concluded the only logical place to begin would be to build a Contracts System first. Selling this idea was going to be at best a very hard sell; however Dick seemed to remember a few short years before he had sold a system to NASA that made this system seem like kindergarten. Actually, after he made his case and pointed out all of the benefits versus the drawbacks he ended up with unanimous support.

After receiving unanimous support to build a complete new system, it was now time to give it a name. Thus, since the contracts were the driving force to everything that followed, the most logical name was Customer Order Requisition Tracking System or CORT. Due to the massive size of the new system it was broken down into several separate and distinct modules, with each module subordinate to the Contracts Module.

The initial staffing for this new system was Mahlon (Dick) Palmer as the Chief Architect and the best programmer that Dick ever worked with, whom he calls John as the Chief Builder (Programmer). Dick was virtually the sole interface with the entire user community and thus wrote essentially all of the system and program specifications. John on the other hand was the primary interface with the entire programming staff and thus was primarily responsible for insuring that all programming was completed in accordance with their new standards. John was also the primary interface with all activities associated with database design. There were numerous other programmers that worked on the project; however there was one other programmer that played an extremely important roll, whom we will call Bill, a name you will hear again.

The first and most critical part of the entire new system was the Contracts Module, a module that must be able to interface with all of the other modules in the new system. Therefore, in order for Dick to get the absolute best information regarding Contracts he needed to locate that one or more persons that totally understood the Contracts Operation, and also understood all of the relationships of the Contracts organization with all other units within the business. Dick found that person whom we will call Judy. Judy and Dick spent many hours together reviewing the many different contracts, of which there were literally hundreds, as well as the many different types of contracts; such as Fixed Price, Progress, Cost Plus, etc. in addition to numerous other types. A major requirement of the new system was to have the ability and the flexibility to accommodate every conceivable type of contract or order, for those unfamiliar with military or government lingo. Dick quickly discovered Judy to be ONE of the most competent people he ever had the opportunity to work with; however there will be several more very competent people that will be identified as they appear in the story.

With Judy's help they designed the entire database structure of the new CORT System, plus all the input screens, the on-line inquiries and all contractually required reporting documents. Dick also discovered that most of the contracts people were very familiar with laptop computers, using much of its associated functionality. One critical piece of functionality that was unique to laptop computers at that time, but was not available using mainframe computers was the ability to preload a computer screen with information that required modifications.

Dick sat down with his top programmer John, and explained this major limitation that was presented by using the mainframe computer. John explained that no such functionality existed on the mainframe that could perform that task. Dick said to John, "Take a week or so and give it some very serious thought, then tell me how we will solve this problem". A few days passed and then one morning John walked into Dick's office with a broad smile on his face and Dick knew he had found a solution. He had the exact solution Dick was looking for. Proof positive he *WAS* the *GREATEST* programmer Dick ever knew.

In addition to the other heavy load of programming, John and his two new recruits also took over the task of designing and building a very sophisticated security system for controlling all access to the new CORT system. This task provided a great training ground for all of them to learn to use the technology that Dick had spent years developing while working for RCA.

The design and development of the CORT System was structured such that as soon as a significant module was thoroughly tested and approved by the user community it could go on line and be implemented. The Utica business became the BETA test site for *all* new modules.

Shortly after the successful implementation of the first and most complicated segment of the CORT system, Dick received a call from the Corporate Auditors out of Division Headquarters that were located in Valley Forge, Pennsylvania. As it turned out they had just finished an audit of a very large mainframe system that the Corporate Center had been commissioned to build. That system was being built to control all aspects of the Corporate Accounting operation. According to the Auditors the Corporate System was somewhat less than a smashing success.

Apparently the Corporate system had been developed using the traditional methodology in vogue at that time, namely the project was separated into numerous smaller activities, each staffed by well-educated individuals who were experts in their particular realm of responsibility. In fact they told us they had run a major test over a week end where they brought all of the smaller segments together for the first time, only to find out that essentially many parts did not fit. They also implied that funding was not considered to be a significant issue.

Later on during their review the auditors requested that Dick give them copies of all of their documentation to include file layouts, report layouts and most importantly copies of all program specifications. Dick's first question was, what did they need all that information for? The reply that Dick received was that they would compare the program specifications to the actual program to insure the program was doing what was intended. Dick's next question was how they would transport all of that program documentation back to Valley Forge. In our brief cases was their confident reply. When Dick told them they would need a large trunk just to pack them in, this was more than they could comprehend. Dick then had to explain to them that there were literally hundreds of programs and that each program had a detailed specification that outlined every input, output, links to applicable database elements plus every decision that the program was required to make. Needless to say they were speechless.

Dick then made them an offer which absolutely astounded them. In lieu of hard copy paper Dick then offered them real-time access to all of this information, in their office in Valley Forge. That completely blew their minds.

They told us that when they audited Valley Forge's super Accounting system if they got a hand written note they considered it fortunate. Dick eventually heard through the grape vine that the corporate system was totally abandoned. Needless to say their new CORT system was off to a very good start.

It is now time to give a more detailed description of the CORT System. The primary driver of the CORT System was the Contracts Module, the software that controls *every activity* that has any relationship to one or more contracts within any given business. Whenever a Site decided to begin using the CORT System it was necessary to first allocate and build the required database structure on the designated mainframe hardware and then assign all the programs that would be necessary to provide the required functionality. Once the software was all in place it was then time for the business to populate the new system with *all* of the Contract information for each and every active contract in the business. This data would be required to produce the many output products that the system was about to produce, such as; Shipping Documents, Shipment Billing Documents, Cost Plus Billing Documents, Progress Billing Documents and Export Control Documents to name a few. In essence, the details of every active contract within the business needed to be loaded into the system in order to receive the maximum benefits that the new system could and would provide.

Since each of the following software sub-modules directly required information from its applicable contract, or updated the contract in some manner Dick will briefly describe each module or sub system. The sequence of development and implementation of each module was determined by the user community and was primarily based on the overall benefits to the businesses.

The first module to be designed and built (after the Primary Contracts Module) was the Shipping Module. This Module directly produced either a government Shipping Document (DD form 250) or a standard commercial Shipping Document for all others. The system determined which document was required based on the contract and ultimately updated the contract accordingly.

The second module to be built was the Shipment Billing Module that produced the appropriate completed Shipment Billing document based on contract specifications. In addition, this module directly interfaced with the Credit and Collections system that Dick had previously built when he first joined Lockheed Martin a year or so previously. With these two systems working in unison it was now possible to make a shipment in the morning and have the government payment in the bank by the following morning. For those of you who understand float you will quickly understand the benefits of this new process. Before CORT was developed it was very common for this same cycle to take as much as thirty days, with a very large staff of typists needed to prepare the final documents.

The third module to be built was a Module that produced Progress Billing Invoices for all applicable Contracts on a cyclical basis. Dick is not going to attempt to explain this process in the limited space we have due to its complexity.

The forth module to be built was a Module that produced Fixed Price Billing Invoices for all Contracts that were appropriately identified. Again Dick will not attempt to explain the complexities of the process.

The final module to be built was the International Compliance Module that maintained control and accountability of all shipments that required Export Licenses. Numerous businesses relied heavily on foreign trade, thus these shipments required very special processing, controls and documentation. This module automatically eliminated much of that additional manual labor. Incidentally, the primary source for virtually all technical information regarding International Compliance was provided by the International Expert from the Orlando, Florida business whom we will call Gloria. Gloria was to International Compliance the same as Judy was to contracts and contracting. Both were extremely knowledgeable in their fields and both an absolute pleasure to work with.

By 1986 the Contracts Portion of the CORT system was now fully operational in the Utica plant, with much interest by Syracuse,

Binghamton and Burlington, Vermont. During this time period the plant in Daytona, Florida found out about the system and requested a full blown demonstration and a detailed presentation of all of CORT's functionality. This presentation became the blueprint for many that would follow over the next couple of years.

The Daytona business, soon to be consolidated with the business that was located in Orlando would then become the second prime mover for the new Shipping system module that Dick was just starting to design. If you remember it was the Shipping system that Dick was initially tasked to build, but after much research convinced management to build the Contracts module first. As it turned out, that became the absolute correct strategy as you will see as we go forward. In addition, getting the Daytona/Orlando business involved at that time also proved extremely beneficial.

The very successful visit from the Corporate Auditors also became a God Send, maybe even "DESTINY" because they provided a tremendous amount of positive press every place they went.

As soon as the shipping module became operational it was immediately installed in the newly combined Orlando Business, immediately replacing an extremely labor intensive task as literally hundreds of shipping documents needed to be manually typed prior to actually making the shipment. In addition there were two types of documents required; the first and most frequently used document was the Government DD Form 250 and the standard generic shipping document that was used for all commercial activity. If you remember the first system that Dick built for GE/Lockheed Martin was a new Credit and Collections system which this system seamlessly connected into, thus providing another major cash flow improvement.

With the Contracts module and now the Shipping module operational there was a major clamor by many Businesses to get on board. Not only that, there were still several major modules that the company still wanted to build that included; Shipment Billing, Cost Plus Billing, Progress Billing, and International Compliance.

Dick also began spending a significant amount of time on the road discussing the new system with perspective new users. These trips usually included a Manager of Finance and/or a Contracts Manager from an operational Site. A typical (SALES) meeting would usually take one to two days to cover all of the system functionality plus Dick gave them live demonstrations of many aspect of the live system. These meetings were generally attended by the site Managers of Finance, Contracts, Shipping, Billing and I am sure on occasion they even brought along the janitor.

As the popularity of the CORT System grew several businesses decided to form a group that called themselves, The CORT Council, a group that initially included a key Contracts Manager from the Syracuse business whom we will call Joe and a second Contracts Manager from the Orlando business that we will call William.

A typical meeting would normally have the attendees arrive at the designated location the evening before the meeting to socialize and get to know each other as each meeting almost always contained several new participants. These meetings were usually well attended by both management and the actual users of CORT.

The actual meeting would begin bright and early the next morning with all of management gathering in one large room and the hands-on users would gather in a separate room. John and his top assistant programmer Bill would usually take all of the actual users into one or more separate rooms for hands-on training. The groups would be divided up based on experience with the system, such as first time users, experienced users, and etcetera.

The main meeting was always chaired by Dick and would usually consist of all Management AND invited potential new users. Any potential problems, either real or perceived were discussed in great detail, suggested improvements were debated and scheduled releases of future modules or enhancements were discussed. Over the course of time this group became a very close knit organization.

Typically the meeting would break up in time so everyone could catch their transportation home that evening.

In the latter part of 1996 Dick was beginning to wind down his career at Lockheed Martin, as well as his computer career which began totally by accident in 1960 and lasted for a total of thirty-six years.

Also in 1996 Lockheed Martin received new management in the world of computers and the new manager was determined to bring LM's systems development technology into the twenty-first century. Dick believes he was an engineer by trade and he wanted to begin by using generally accepted engineering practices in the world of systems design. Dick can understand his frustrations since throughout all of his years at LM he had never seen ANY computer system, other than the CORT system, and all other systems that were designed and built there by Dick that had any structure, what-so-ever.

Dick was invited to a management meeting that detailed how LM's management would quickly show immediate progress towards this new goal. In essence they had decided to reverse engineer a couple of very simple systems by creating all of the missing documents and making it appear like progress. During the meeting Dick proposed that instead of using reverse engineering *to give the illusion* of making progress that they simply use the CORT system *in total to prove* they had a system in place that nearly met ALL of the criteria that was outlined in the new directive. In addition, CORT was the largest system ever developed within Lockheed Martin Corporation. At first they could not, nor would not believe that statement to be true, however after a very lengthy review they collectively agreed CORT did in fact meet nearly every requirement.

Dick's further recommendation was to have one of their new hot shot programmers, namely Bill work with Dick to identify any deficiencies and make the necessary corrections. The most common deficiency was the absence of signoff approvals when the completed product was installed; however they had approvals for all of the design criteria throughout the development cycle. The new directive wanted final approvals as well.

Six months or so after Dick retired; one of the Managers contacted Dick in an effort to determine where he had found such a complete plan for systems development. The caller indicated they had searched all conceivable places with no success. At that time Dick told him the entire plan was developed over the years and resided solely in his head. Dick further told him he had used this methodology to design complete systems for the Air Force (BMEWS and the Dew Line in the Arctic), NAVY (AUTEC in the Bahamas), NASA (Apollo Mission Warehouse, in Baltimore, Maryland) and numerous Accounting and Payroll Systems as well as many more too numerous to mention.

Incidentally, earlier in this writing Dick has divulged his methodology for the first time since he began developing it in 1962 but there is more to the story so this is a good place to tell you the *REST OF THE STORY.*

When Dick went to work for RCA Service Company in 1961 as an Electronics Accounting Machine (EAM) Operator, he had a grand total of less than <u>eight</u> hours of higher education, and student loans totaling nearly $150 (yes one hundred fifty dollars) all at the Utica School of Commerce. It was there where he had learned how to operate EAM (Electronic Accounting Machine) equipment after leaving the Air Force, and up until that time he had never even heard of computers. He first discovered EAM equipment completely by accident while eating his lunch during a period of time when he was working for a Heavy Equipment Dealer in Utica, New York. As he was eating his lunch he was just killing time by randomly thumbing through an old phone book when he stumbled upon an advertisement for the Utica School of Commerce. It was at that moment that *"DESTINY"* took over and completely changed his life and as they say, "The Rest Is History"

Virtually everything Dick has done from that time forward has been self-taught. He began programming on the IBM 650 computer, using SOAPII, next on to the IBM 1401 using Assembly Language; then RCA 70/15 using Assembly Language; then CDC3400 Using COBOL; then RCA 70/45 using COBOL and IDMS. Now, Dick has trouble making a PC work, getting old sure is tough!

Using those computers and software, Dick has built computer systems from PC size to the largest business systems in RCA at NASA, that controlled all aspects of their very large warehouse in Baltimore,

Maryland, a system that supported the entire Apollo Mission; and then on to Lockheed Martin where he built the largest Accounting System (named CORT) in Lockheed Martin Corporation at that time. From the first time he saw the IBM 650 computer when he went to work for RCA he was determined that he would master that MONSTER one way or another. He had no mentor or teacher, so as you do when growing up on the farm; many times you have no help or guidance so you just figure it out and get the job done. That philosophy has served him very, very well throughout his entire computer career; therefore, all he knows now about computers and system design, *HE JUST FIGURED IT OUT.*

Remember way back in this story, Dick told about volunteering for a job that required designing and building an Inventory Control system on a very large NAVY contract, known as AUTEC (Atlantic Underwater Test and Evaluation Center) that was located on Andros Island in the Bahama Islands. At the time he volunteered for that job he had never even designed a Computer program, much less a complete Inventory Control System.

While writing this story, it has given Dick much time to reflect back on events that had a significant impact on his life and more importantly on his career. The AUTEC experience was one of those events. When he was given the task, he had a very short period of time to develop a plan which took him back to his days on the farm where he normally had a very short period of time to develop a workable solution. Those experiences again served him well.

In fact, the original solution that Dick developed to solve the AUTEC problem worked so well, Dick adopted it as the basis that he used for the remainder of his entire career that spanned some thirty-five years. Sure, he made some enhancements along the way, but the original philosophy was sound and never changed. I guess it was just "DESTINY".

Looking back on the AUTEC experience, Dick finds it very difficult to understand how three very high level and outstanding managers (including two VP's), within the organization even gave Dick any consideration at all, much less gave him the job. Maybe it was desperation where everyone else was smart enough to refuse the task. In any case, that opportunity turned into the "Second Greatest Gift of His Life". You may remember the first greatest gift was passing his induction physical when joining the Air Force when he should have failed it.

The number of systems that Dick used his new found methodology in developing are far too many to list here, however, they include; Payroll, Accounts Payable, Accounts Receivable, Inventory Control for BMEWS and DEW Line, Inventory Control for over one hundred NASA Tracking Stations around the world, including the warehouse in Baltimore, Maryland that supported them, and lastly the largest business system ever developed in the Lockheed Martin Corporation up to that time known as CORT.

As you may have noticed above Dick has built computer systems in nearly every discipline possible, therefore he needed to find a way that a dumb farm kid like him could master all of that information and convert it into a sophisticated computer system without taking time out to go to college to get a degree. Remember NECESSITY IS THE MOTHER OF ALL INVENTIONS. Also take a look at history and you will discover that nearly all significant inventions were built by people without a formal education because they had not yet learned that what they wanted to do was impossible to do, so they just went ahead and built it anyway.

Now it is time to provide a few details about the CORT System.

-CORT stands for Customer Order Requisition Tracking and is a Computer System that controls all aspects of a Customer Order from receipt of the order (Contract) to final closeout.

When was it built? Initial planning, and approval to build the system began in 1985 and the first Module, referred to as the Contracts Module, was built and became operational in 1986 in the Utica, New York GE/LM plant. The Utica plant was the Beta test site for all modules as they became available.

How large was the system?

A total of approximately twenty businesses within Lockheed

Martin used the system throughout its life cycle.

There are nearly one million lines of system/program specifications.

There are nearly one million lines of JCL (Job Control Language).

There are approximately two million lines of program code.

The system was first implemented in 1986 and is still operational 30 years later. A relative description of the entire system was given previously so no more details are required here. However, as more and more businesses decided to use the system the new users wanted to get more involved in the decision making process.

Whenever a Site decided to begin using the CORT System it was necessary to first allocate and build the required database structure on the designated mainframe hardware, and then assign all the programs that would be necessary to provide the required functionality.

One of the first businesses to become interested in the CORT System following the successful implementation in Utica was the business located in Daytona Beach, Florida. The Contracts Organization in Orlando was managed by a fellow we will call William, who would become a critical piece of the CORT Steering Committee throughout the development and implementation cycle. However, at this point he had just started to hear about CORT and wanted more information, in fact much more info.

In order to satisfy the Daytona request for more information that would detail the complexities of the CORT (Customer Order Requisition Tracking) system Dick put together a very comprehensive slide presentation that explained the inner workings of the system. Since the Contracts portion of the system was all that was operational at that time, this presentation concentrated on the many relationships between Requisitions, Customer Names and Order Numbers and all the many other relationships that are maintained by the system. This presentation also concentrated on how these many relationships would be used in future modules.

With a system this large and one operating in such a diverse environment, it was absolutely critical that all businesses that were going to implement CORT must agree to standardize their terminology to that used by CORT. Those meetings frequently resulted in some very heated debates.

One of the early businesses to show a great deal of interest in the system was the Aircraft Business located in Marietta, Georgia. A rather large group of CORT users were invited to their plant for initial conversations. A part of that visit included a tour of their manufacturing facility. It was quite an operation, to say the least. The manufacturing building (all situated under one roof) contained four assembly lines. In just half of the building there was an assembly line for C-130 aircraft in every stage of development from just the wheels to completed aircraft ready to go out the door. As Dick remembers there were probably at least twenty or more aircraft in various stages of assembly. The other assembly line was manufacturing F-35 Fighters (I believe) all under heavy security and wraps.

This meeting lasted pretty much the entire day with the recipients showing much interest.

Finally, like all other things, it was now time to hang up the old antique spurs and put the aging old Stallion out to pasture. Thus in January 1997 Dick attended his final CORT Council meeting. This meeting just happened to be held in Valley Forge, Pennsylvania.

As had happened many times before, Dick along with John and Bill flew to Philadelphia where the meeting would be held in Valley Forge. A very good longtime friend, whom we will call the Colonel from Orlando, had made arrangements to take Dick to a very unique store in Downtown Philly that specialized in every kind of model imaginable. As Dick remembers the store was several floors high with each floor specializing in a different kind of model; in the meantime the other two guys took a cab to the hotel where they would await the arrival of the Colonel and Dick.

Finally at around 2000 hours (8:00PM) the Colonel suggested that they should probably head back to the hotel and meet the other two guys for dinner. When they got to the hotel lobby they met the other guys and they all headed to the restaurant for dinner.

When they walked into the restaurant they found the room was packed with friends of Dicks' from all over the country whom he had had very close working relationships throughout his many years with both RCA and then the past fifteen or more years with Lockheed Martin. To say the least Dick was nearly in shock. The celebrating went on throughout dinner.

After dinner was over the party finally began. The Colonel was the Master of Ceremonies and he introduced many speakers. Dick didn't even know he knew so many people, much less that they had so many complementary things to say. Those attendees ranged from data inputters to high level Managers. After the speeches were over they then brought out all kinds of gifts and memorabilia. The party finally broke up about midnight.

The next morning it was time to get back to work as usual. The crowd was a little larger than normal, but certainly not unusual. As usual John and Bill took all of the people that made the system run; and then separated them into two groups based on system experience, etc. The large remaining group that stayed with Dick was primarily made up of Management and a couple of groups of potential new users. In essence the meeting was going like dozens before. Suddenly a longtime friend, whom we will call Harry, had taken over the meeting. Harry and Dick had worked very closely back in the RCA days at Cherry Hill, NJ many years ago.

Harry now appeared to be in charge and he was taking over as Master of Ceremonies of yet another party. They had goodies to eat and drink, then more speeches and then they presented Dick with more gifts. This time the gifts were all from the old RCA gift shop. The gifts included an RCA hat and a special RCA jacket with 'HIS MASTER'S VOICE' logo embroidered on the front along with many other items. Finally the meeting (party) broke up and everyone returned home.

Later in the week, Thursday morning, January 30, 1997 began like virtually all January 30ths would have begun for decades before; however this January 30th would become different. Basically, Dick had been employed since he joined the Air Force in 1954 and had essentially been working ever since. Thus, beginning tomorrow, January 31, 1997 he would no longer be employed. But for now it was time to enjoy this day.

The day began very much like the many days before, first a cup of coffee to get the old wheels turning, and then time to discuss the agenda for the day with a line of people who needed guidance. John and Bill had their usual questions since they were still engaged in making the CORT system completely in compliance with the new upper level management decision to make at least one system totally compliant. Incidentally, the CORT system is the only system in Lockheed Martin Corporation that ever met that objective that this writer is aware of.

Suddenly it became apparent that more than the normal amount of traffic was starting to gather, people from Finance, Contracts, Engineering, Manufacturing and then people from the Syracuse plant, and Binghamton and then some people that Dick did not even know.

Well it soon became apparent that another retirement party was in the making. This was completely overwhelming. Again there were speeches and gifts and good wishes for the future. This was all just mind boggling. How could the accomplishments of a simple farm boy with no formal education be recognized and appreciated by so many people?

Chapter Eight

RETIREMENT

On July 31, 2014 at around 1630 hours, or 4:30 PM Dick had a massive heart attack while helping his friend Mary pick up after a long day at the Clinton, NY Farmers Market. As a direct result of a very rapid response by the Clinton Fire department and a comparable response by the heart unit at Saint Elizabeth Hospital he was able to write this book. In fact, the writing of this book was the direct result of a suggestion by one of the Cardiac Nurses in Saint Elizabeth Hospital to whom he will forever be grateful.

As you may have noticed; travel has been a major part of Dick's life since the day he left the farm when he was just barely seventeen years old. Not much has changed over the years, however there are still a few places left to visit. Therefore, it doesn't appear that he will run out of opportunities in the foreseeable future.

The following is a partial list of major National Parks and other notable places that Dick has visited throughout his travels. Many of these parks have also been visited by his good friend, Mary.

Acadia National Park, Maine

Allegheny Potage Railroad Historic Site, Pennsylvania

America's Stonehenge, New Hampshire

Antietam National Battlefield, Maryland

Arches National Park, Utah

Badlands National Park, North Dakota

Banff National Park, British Columbia, Canada

Big Hole National Battlefield, Montana

Big South Fork National Recreation Area, Tennessee

Bingham Canyon Open Pit Copper Mine, N.H.L. Utah

Black Canyon of the Gunnison N.P. Colorado

Blue Ridge Mountains National Parkway

Bryce Canyon National Park, Utah

Canyonlands National Park, Utah

Carlsbad Caverns National Park, New Mexico

Chesapeake and Ohio Canal National Historic Park, Md.

Colorado National Monument, Colorado

Columbia Ice Field, British Columbia, Canada

Crater Lake National Park, Oregon

Craters of the Moon National Monument, Idaho

Crazy Horse Monument, South Dakota

Custer State Park, South Dakota

Death Valley National Park, California

Denali National Park and Preserve, Alaska

Deschutes National Forest, Oregon

Devils Tower National Monument, Wyoming

Fetterman's Battlefield, Wyoming

Fort Clatsop National Memorial (Lewis & Clark), Oregon

Fort Laramie National Historic Site, Wyoming

Fortress of Louisburg, Nova Scotia, Canada

Four Corners - Arizona, Colorado, New Mexico and Utah

Fundy National Park, New Brunswick, Canada

Garden of the Gods, Colorado

Gates of the Mountains Wilderness Area, Montana

Gettysburg Memorial Park, Pennsylvania

Glacier National Park, Montana

Glen Canyon National Recreation Area, Utah

Golden Spike National Historic Site, Utah

Grand Canyon National Park, Arizona

Grand Staircase National Monument, Escalante, Utah

Grand Teton National Park, Wyoming

Great Salt Lake, Utah

Great Sand Dunes National Park, Colorado

Harpers Ferry Historical Park, West Virginia

Hells Canyon National Recreation Area, Oregon & Wash.

Hopewell Culture Historic Park, Ohio

Ivvavik National Park of Canada

Jamestown National Historic Park, Virginia

Jefferson National Expansion Memorial, Missouri

Johnstown Flood National Memorial, Pennsylvania

Joshua Tree National Park, California

Kings Canyon National Park, California

Knife River Indian Villages Historic Park, N. Dakota

Lassen Volcanic National Park, California

Lewis and Clark Expedition – Many Sites

Lighthouses – Many in the U.S. and Canada

Little Bighorn Battlefield National Monument, Montana

Luray Caverns, Virginia

Mammoth Cave National Park, Kentucky

Manassas National Battlefield, Virginia

Medicine Wheel National Historic Site, Wyoming

Mesa Verde National Park, Colorado

Mission Ruins – Many in the Southwest U.S.

Missouri River Breaks National Monument, Montana

Monument Valley, Utah

Monticello, Virginia

Mount Rainier National Park, Washington

Mount Rushmore Memorial, South Dakota

Mt St. Helens National Volcanic Monument, Washington

Mount Washington, New Hampshire

National Cathedral, Washington, D.C.

National Petroleum Reserve in Alaska

Natural Bridge, Virginia

Newberry National Monument, Oregon

Open Pit Coal Mine, New Mexico

Oregon Trail – Many Sites

Organ Pipe Cactus National Monument, Arizona

Picture Rocks National Lakeshore, Michigan

Pikes Peak, Colorado

Rock of Ages Granite Quarry, New Hampshire

Rocky Mountain National Park, Colorado

Royal Gorge, Colorado

Saguaro National Park, Arizona

Salinas Pueblo Missions National Monument, Arizona

Scotts Bluff National Monument & Devils Gate, Nebraska

Sequoia National Park, California

Shelburne Museum, Vermont

Sleeping Bear Dunes National Lakeshore, Michigan

Steam Town National Historic Site, Pennsylvania

Temple Square, Salt Lake City, Utah

National Mall, Washington, D.C.

Theodore Roosevelt National Park, North Dakota

UFO Museum, Roswell, New Mexico

White Sands National Monument, New Mexico

Yellowstone National Park, Wyoming

Yorktown National Historic Park, Virginia

Yosemite National Park, California

Zion National Park, Utah

Although the above locations represent travel, which essentially was done after Dick retired from Lockheed Martin in 1997, there was much travel that was done before Dick's wife, Joy Ann's health deteriorated to a point where she was not able to travel.

Dicks travelling days essentially began almost the day he joined the Air Force, for up until that time he had barely been out of Delaware County, New York where he grew up on the family farm. For example, after Dick joined the Air Force in 1954, and then was married in 1957, it was at that time when his travelling became a serious endeavor, with his first married assignment being at Homestead AFB on the southern tip of Florida. Following his discharge from the Air Force, Dick and his wife purchased a house in Remsen, New York. After joining RCA Service Company, Dick worked at Griffiss AFB in Rome, New York where he worked for a couple of years, and then he ultimately accepted a promotion that transferred him to Cherry Hill, New Jersey where he remained for approximately three years.

From Cherry Hill he accepted another promotion that transferred him to Baltimore, Maryland where he worked on a contract that operated a large warehouse for NASA. Dick's next move resulted from another promotion that took him to Colorado Springs, Colorado where he worked on the BMEWS and DEW Line contracts for three more years.

When those contracts folded, Dick accepted a layoff from RCA and moved back to Clinton, New York where he ultimately joined Lockheed Martin where his moving days came to an end.

Moving from state to state became grueling, however it did give him the opportunity to travel extensively.

Photographing the Louis and Clark Expedition;

As you can see Dick has travelled extensively; however, one trip in particular has been exceptional, or maybe it should be described more accurately as a series of trips that occurred over a period of several years. The trip that Dick is speaking of is travelling the ENTIRE Lewis and Clark Trail. Many of those trips occurred during the Bi-Centennial celebration which lasted from 2003 through 2006.

Contrary to popular knowledge (opinion) the story begins at President Jefferson's home at Monticello where much of the planning with his close friend and neighbor, Meriwether Lewis took place and ends in Tennessee where Meriwether Lewis committed suicide, or as some historians believe was murdered.

There are important parts of this story that have intentionally been omitted since several particular locations contain no remaining known structure or object that is photographable. One such location is in the city of Pittsburg, Pennsylvania where the famous keel boat was built.

As you read the story please keep in mind this is being written primarily from memory, much of which may be fifteen or more years old. Thus the story may not be one hundred percent historically accurate, therefore the purpose is to simply get you from one photo opportunity to the next.

This story is written chronologically; thus it may differ slightly from what is generally accepted as fact. History states the expedition began in 1803 which is true and lasted until 1806, or did it end on October 11, 1809 when Lewis committed suicide in Tennessee? Or was Lewis murdered in Tennessee as some historians believe. In either case there are markers in Tennessee identifying the location of the tragedy.

During the July 4th, 1803 celebration, President Jefferson announced the United States had just purchased the land that is today commonly known as the Louisiana Purchase. Immediately following those ceremonies Lewis headed south to the Harpers Ferry Armory to pick up the supplies needed for the expedition, such as guns, ammo, tomahawks and a collapsible boat.

The next stop on our journey is a place called Falls of the Ohio, located nearly across the Ohio River from what is now Louisville, Kentucky. Louis would meet William Clark at the home of his brother, General George Rogers Clark to form the core of the Louis and Clark expedition. However it is here that a major discrepancy exists with the story about Louis and Clark. William Clark was not allowed to return to the Army with his previous rank of Captain but rather as a Lieutenant. Therefore, there was only one Captain on the expedition; however no one ever knew about this fact and Clark was always treated as a Captain. For the sake of accuracy this story will refer to Captain Louis and Lieutenant Clark as co-Commanders and NOT as co-Captains.

On October 26, 1803 the co-Commanders Lewis and Clark began their epic journey down the Ohio River to explore the Louisiana Purchase and the Pacific Northwest. Prior to this journey the Commanders had been seeking and finding young men to join the Army. Qualifications were strict: Un- married, no children, river/ boating skills, hunting skills, Indian fighting skills and woodsman skills.

On December 12, 1803 Commander Clark and his ruffian group of new recruits landed at Wood's River near Cahokia, Illinois where they began building Camp River Dubois. The expedition spent the winter at this site where Commander Clark changed this rag-tag group of recruits into some semblance of an Army organization. On May 14, 1804 the Corps of Discovery departed Camp Dubois to begin their western expedition.

The Corps of Discovery stopped in St. Charles, Missouri for about a week to complete some business. The old part of town is much the same as it was at the time of the expedition with much to see and photograph.

As you travel north you will pass the confluences of the Platte and Missouri Rivers as mentioned in the Journals, then you will reach Sioux City, Iowa. It is here that Sergeant Charles Floyd died on August 20th, 1804, most likely from a ruptured appendix. Sergeant Floyd would be the only member of the expedition to die. There are numerous places to visit and photograph in that area.

The next stop was at Spirit Mound near Vermillion, South Dakota. The Indians believed this mound was inhabited by very small people that could kill at great distances, thus it should be checked out by members of the expedition. No unusual people were found. On August 26, 1804 members of the Corp hiked to the top, as did we. The view is also spectacular and Clark indicated they could see buffalo in every direction as far as the eye could see. While at the top Dick and Mary met a man from Arkansas who was also travelling the Lewis and Clark Trail. Upon returning to the parking lot some mile or so away, Dick introduced him to one of their dogs who was travelling with them. Her name was Sacajawea and he was so impressed he needed to get all kinds of photographs.

On September 25, 1804 Lewis and Clark met with the Teton Sioux Indians at the mouth of the Bad River, so named because of this meeting. This meeting nearly resulted in a deadly face-off, however the Indians finally stood down and the expedition passed without further incident.

Moving further up river to Mobridge, SD you will find much Western Indian history plus a large monument commemorating Sacajawea.

On October 26, 1804 the expedition reached a place near what is now known as Mandan, North Dakota (then inhabited by the Mandan Indians).

Incidentally the Indian population in this general area was decimated by the white mans' diseases as evidenced by the many village ruins. Near Camp Mandan was a large Mandan Indian village that was nearly wiped out in 1781 by a devastating small pox epidemic that killed three quarters of the population. Many signs of that village still remain.

It was near there that the expedition built their winter quarters known as Fort Mandan, with building of the fort beginning on November 2nd and being occupied on November 16th. Many significant events occurred here which had major impacts on the future of the expedition. Most importantly, Sacajawea and her husband Toussaint Charbonneau joined the Expedition. Before departing in the spring Sacajawea would give birth to their son, Jon Baptiste, also affectionately known by Clark as Pompey. Clark calculated they had travelled some 1600 miles since leaving Camp Dubois. Sometime probably in early May 1805 the expedition departed Fort Mandan.

In late May 1805 the Corp of Discovery passed through what is known today as the Missouri River Breaks. This section of the river provides some exceptionally spectacular photo opportunities, EXCEPT it is extremely difficult to reach. Expect much serious planning before you start.

After passing through the Breaks the river turns sharply to the south and this part of the river begins to go through the mountains. By this time you will fast be approaching Great Falls, Montana, one of the most difficult challenges that the expedition would face. There is much to see and do in Great Falls since this is the home of the most spectacular Louis and Clark Interpretive Center in the country. Dick and Mary have visited it at least three times.

While searching for a route through the Great Falls area Clark discovered a giant spring that produces 134,000 gallons of water per minute and is the head waters for the world's shortest river, the Roe River with a total length of only 200 feet.

On July 19, 1805 the expedition entered an area that they named "The Gates of the Mountains". The river channel is 6.5 miles in length and is exactly the same width as the river. Some of the cliffs reach a towering 1200 feet high and are located just north of Helena, Montana.

The expedition reached the three forks of the Missouri on July 25, 1805. It was in this area that Sacajawea first recognized parts of the landscape from her childhood from some five years previous, when she was kidnapped by the Hidatsa Indians and taken back to the Dakotas. It is generally accepted that she was most likely about twelve or thirteen years old when she joined the Expedition and most likely did not act as a guide to the expedition as some historians would have you believe. Remember she had most likely not been in these areas since she was a child.

On August 8, 1805 Sacajawea recognized a prominent land mark that she remembered as the Beaver's Head. It was probably in this small area that Sacajawea acquired the reputation as being a guide to the Expedition.

On or about August 9, 1805 Captain Lewis and a few other men met Chief Comeahwait and about sixty Shoshone warriors. These were the people of Sacajawea and the Indian tribe the expedition had been searching for.

On August 12, 1805 Lewis first reached the summit of Lemhi Pass, a point where Lewis would leave the Missouri River Basin and witness the broad expanse of the Rocky Mountains that they must traverse before reaching their destination of the Pacific Ocean. That view was a very disheartening revelation. Incidentally no one on the expedition had ever seen mountains like the ones they were going to need to cross. Remember it was generally believed that the Missouri river would connect to the Columbia River after a very short portage as the western mouth of that river was well known by traders, thus the sinking feeling felt by Lewis from the summit of Lemhi Pass.

On August 13, 1805 Lewis and Clark met with Chief Comeahwait, who while during negotiations Sacajawea recognized him as her brother whom she had not seen since she was kidnapped several years previously. Prior to this event the expedition was not going to get the needed horses, thus this one event was the complete game changer for the success of the entire expedition. As a result of that fortuitous meeting, the Corp of Discovery negotiated the purchase of horses that were needed to complete the expedition. Incidentally, this area was the birth place of Sacajawea and there is much to see in the area.

Winter was closing in quickly while travelling on the Lolo Trail where the expedition nearly starved to death, thus they needed to eat one of their horses to prevent starvation. This short distance was one of the most difficult of the total expedition.

On September 20 1805 the Corp of Discovery made first contact with the Nez Perce Indians. There is much history with that historic meeting. They made friends with the Nez Perce and ultimately left their horses with them to be picked up in the spring on their return trip home. Since the remainder of the journey would be on the Columbia River they would need to build dugout canoes. All able bodied men built five dugout canoes from September 27, 1805 until October 7, 1805 when they were ready to depart on the final leg of the journey.

In early October 1805 the Corp of Discovery finally reached the Columbia River. Clark spotted what he believed was Mount Saint Helens on October 18, 1805; however todays geographers believe he was looking at Mt Adams.

On November 7, 1805 Clark wrote, "Great joy in camp, we are in view of the Ocean (Pacific)".

On or about November tenth through fifteenth the expedition camped on the northern bank of the Columbia while deciding where to spend the winter. That decision was made by taking a vote of all members, INCLUDING both Sacajawea and York, making them both the first woman and first black to vote in the new nation. Note: York was Clark's personal slave.

The decision was made to build a Fort on the south side of the river with building starting on December 8, 1805. The Fort was named Fort Clatsop after the Clatsop Indians and they moved into the Fort on Christmas Eve. They remained at the fort for a total of 106 days with rain every day but twelve. They departed Fort Clatsop on March 23, 1806.

Dick's photos of Fort Clatsop were taken sometime during the bi-centennial celebration; however sometime after that the original replica fort burnt to the ground and then was rebuilt. The date of that fire is unknown.

During the winter Captain Clark calculated the distance they had travelled since leaving St Louis. He will need to work on those skills since he calculated a total of 4168 miles. Using modern technology they have determined he was off by less than 40 miles.

On the return trip Lewis and nine other men left the main party and headed northeast to explore the Marias River area. Lewis and his men would reach their furthest point north as evidenced by an appropriate marker. Meanwhile Captain Clark and the rest of the Expedition would head Southeast to locate and explore the Yellowstone River.

On July 26, 1806 Lewis and his men had a confrontation with eight Blackfeet Indians. While the Indians were trying to steal their horses, a battle ensued and two Indians were killed, the only deaths from hostilities on the entire expedition.

Clark, while exploring the Yellowstone River, discovered a large sandstone formation that had been a landmark for generations. Clark named this formation 'Pompey's Pillar" after Sacajawea's son whom Clark affectionately called Pompey. This pillar is VERY unique in that it contains the only known indication "anyplace" that the Core of Discovery had passed that way. This inscription is Clarks signature which is heavily guarded and protected. Incidentally the formation is located near Custer, Montana.

The expedition came back together west of Fort Mandan, and then returned to Saint Louis, completing the journey in September 1806.

The previous description of the Louis and Clark journey leaves out much, if not most of the details of the expedition; however it is only an attempt to identify, describe and locate the major points of interest along the route.

There are however two other events that must be addressed. Sacajawea was a very unique young lady since she must have died at least three times. How so you may ask. Well she is buried in three different places around the country as evidenced by Dick's photographs.

In their travels to visit ALL significant sites on the Lewis and Clark trail, they have visited the two sites that have markers identifying the burial sites of Sacajawea and the third site, Fort Manual, in what is now known as Kenel, where it was recorded in their journals that she died. Now back to the real sub-story.

The closest camp ground to Kenel was in Mobridge, SD where Dick and Mary arrived late on a Saturday evening. Early Sunday morning their plan was to head north to Kennel and locate Fort Manual. Sunday morning brought very heavy rains and they could not locate Fort Manual thus they stopped at a very small gas station to get directions. The gas station was also a very small convenience store, operated by two rather elderly ladies. While asking for directions the ladies casually asked where Dick and Mary were from. The conversation went something like so:

Ladies: "Where are you from"?

Dicks reply: "New York"

Ladies: "But where in New York?"

Quite frankly Dick thought she was jerking his chain. This line of questioning went on a bit more and she finally found out they lived in Clinton, NY.

It turned out her daughter had lived in Clinton at one time and had worked there as a nurse in the Slocome-Dixon clinic.

We were now old friends and were invited to sit down and enjoy a cup of coffee. They told us they had a story to tell us, a story about their family.

Apparently many years before, their great grand-father was a Bootlegger on the Missouri River, running liquor to the Indians when there was a boating accident and the entire family was killed except for one very small boy. This little boy managed to get to shore and was hiding in a barn when an Indian family found him a day or so later. This Indian family took him in and raised him to adulthood.

When he was more or less grown up, the Indian family told the boy it was time for him to decide if he was going to be an Indian or if he wanted to go back to being a white man. The boy stated he had grown up as an Indian, thus he was going to stay Indian. Incidentally, this boy married an Indian woman with whom they had a son who was these two women's father.

As time passed, World War II came along and the young man was now either inducted or joined the military where he became a CODE TALKER.

Our hosts Wanted to know if we knew what Code Talkers were and Dick said they were Navajo Indians. Our hosts said that was partly true; however many Lakota-Sioux Indians were also Code Talkers and their father was one of them. They said they never knew him well since he died at a very young age from malaria and he had never talked about his experiences in the military.

These ladies further went on to tell them that about a year before that current visit, an official from the military made them a visit and informed them about their father's involvement with the code talkers since it had now all been de-classified. Their hosts informed Dick and Mary they never knew any of this information about their father before that visit.

The ladies also told them that since Dick and Mary were staying in Mobridge that there was a large museum there and if they stopped they could see all of the original documentation. Dick and Mary took the ladies up on their offer and stopped at the Museum that afternoon. Not only did the museum show them the documentation when they stopped, but rather gave them a complete set of copies of everything. Incidentally, since this all happened on Sunday when the Fort was closed, the ladies also invited them back on Monday morning for a private guided tour which they accepted.

The second event involved Captain Lewis when he was recalled to Washington to settle a dispute over funding of the expedition and delays in publishing the journals. While travelling on the Natchez Trace Trail northwest of Lawrenceburg, Tennessee, Lewis committed suicide following a severe case of mental depression. A few historians believe Lewis' death was murder. In either case there are numerous markers in the area.

Other Travel Adventures

When you travel as many miles and visit as many places as Dick has, you too will experience many interesting and unique adventures. In an attempt to whet your appetite for some of these adventures Dick is going to relate several stories that he believes are worth passing on.

The first story takes place in Yellowstone National Park. The year is unknown and is unimportant; however the day was Fourth of July. The crowds were massive, and particularly around Old Faithful when it was scheduled to erupt at around noon. Dick was accompanied by his friend Mary on this trip. Earlier in the morning they had scouted out the lay of the land, looking for the ideal spot to photograph Old Faithful when it erupted. In their search for that ideal spot, they found a trail leading up away from the crowds that appeared to be the perfect spot. The plan was to return to the trail at the appointed time and find that spot.

The plan was working to perfection as the appointed time was close to arrival. Upon their return to the trail head, what should appear right in the trail, but a very large buffalo. So much for a well laid plan, so they settled for joining all of the other visitors. As it turned out, if they would have gone up the trail, the photo(s) they got would not have been visible.

Shortly after finding a new suitable spot, they noticed a patron taking some very up close and personal photos of this big buffalo by kneeling probably some forty or fifty feet directly in front of this very large bull. The photographer had additionally invited his wife and two kids to come down closer to get a better view. Almost simultaneously the big bull began to paw the dirt and snorting very loudly. Dick told Mary to get her camera, as he believed the bull was about to charge.

Before Dick or Mary could get their cameras turned on, the Bull did indeed charge and badly ripped the man's leg open from knee to crotch. It was easy to tell since the man was wearing shorts. The man picked himself up off the ground and began running towards a nearby tree for safety, but he was not quick enough since the bull charged again, this time throwing the man at least six feet into the air from the back.

By this time, many Rangers were attempting to distract the bull while giving the man time enough to crawl behind a tree. All the spectators were immediately herded out of the area, to give the bull as much room as possible as the bull began to settle down.

With the people out of the way, the bull finally ambled over to Old FAITHFUL and once again began eating. Please check the photo section and you will see Old Faithful, in full eruption mode, within minutes after this event, with the bull standing directly in front of Old Faithful.

Incidentally, Dick spoke with a woman Ranger shortly after this event, and she informed Dick that the guy also receive a $1000 citation for harassing the animals. A couple of days later while travelling in the Dakotas, they heard a news report that included an update of this event and the man was still in serious condition. Moral of the story, "Don't MESS WITH THE BUFFALO"!

Dick's next adventure takes place in Glacier National Park. Dick, accompanied by his friend Mary decided bright and early one morning to hike up a fairly long trail to Apikuni Falls. They got to the trail head about 0800 hours, only to find a group already ahead of them; that was being led by a Park Ranger. They were not in the mood to follow along with a group of old people. Little did they realize that someday, they too would get old, but not that day.

Anyway, their plan was to just catch up with them, and then blow by and be on their way. That plan was about to change. The Ranger was a college professor from an upper Midwest University who spent his summers working in the park as a Ranger. He immediately came to the back of the group to welcome us and to invite us to join them.

For some reason, he and Dick just clicked. From then on it was just he and Dick. They had much to talk about, with Dick's entire wilderness backpacking, travelling and so-forth. A woman in the group could not understand how anyone else except the professor could talk about such issues.

The hike was finally over just before lunch and the professor took Mary and Dick aside and confided that he was leading another trip that afternoon which included two boat rides. He stated he would like very much for us to join him if we could. Fortunately, we had nothing specific planned so we took him up on his offer.

The afternoon trip was spectacular and resulted in numerous fantastic photographs.

The real kicker was yet to come. When they got back to the dock the professor offered Dick a full time job as a Park Ranger in Glacier National Park, complete with a place to live, with all of the amenities. The job would begin tomorrow. The professor said it is virtually impossible to find anyone with Dick's experiences. Unfortunately, Dick had way too many obligations back in New York, but what an offer.

This was another adventure; but almost a tragedy. This situation took place in Chama, New Mexico. At that time Dick was training many Service Dogs for the handicapped. So you might ask what is a Service Dog? And more importantly, what can they do? This particular dog was a relatively small Black Labrador Retriever. The following is a partial list of her many capabilities: Open doors, pull wheel chairs, carry objects such as your lunch to the table, clear the table and put garbage in the trash can, take the laundry out of the dryer and place on the bed to name just a few. On this trip Dick and Mary were travelling with Dick's Service Dog, named Bramble, and Brandy which was a small Papillion. These two dogs had travelled many miles with Dick and Mary in the camper, so today was not unusual.

There is a campground at Chama, but more importantly, there is a narrow gauge railroad that has scenic rides between Chama, New Mexico and Antonito, Colorado. They had a full day trip planned that went half way and then returned to Chama. Their plan was to take the day trip, leaving early in the morning and returning late afternoon. As usual the dogs had been left in the camper. It is important to know this all took place in the late fall, thus there were very few people at the campground

After Dick and Mary returned that evening, they were having their dinner when the Campground owner stopped by to see if everything was OK. He was concerned because he thought we had left the camper door open because they had found the two dogs wandering around the park. When checking their tags, they discovered the dogs were from New York, and when they checked our campsite they found the door open, thus they put them back in and relocked the door.

So what really happened? We had forgotten to cover the door lock and knob and Bramble had decided to let themselves out to take a walk to pass the time. Trust me; we were much more careful thereafter as this could have been a very bad tragedy.

In 2005 Dick and Mary decided to travel to the southwest to visit the deserts in New Mexico and Arizona and as expected the deserts were in full bloom, certainly a site to behold. However while they were there, they heard that Death Valley was expecting the Hundred Year bloom due to the unusually early heavy rainfall that year. A quick change in plans was well worth the trip. That was their first trip to Death Valley, but certainly not their last. Over the course of time, Death Valley became their all-time favorite National Park. The question becomes why? If you are a photographer, virtually everything becomes a photo opportunity.

Sometimes when travelling, you just stumble onto an interesting situation. That was the case with this next adventure. Dick and Mary were planning to visit the Custer Battlefield, a short distance north of Harding, Montana. They had picked Harding because there are not a lot of Campgrounds in that part of the country, so they had to take what they could find. When they arrived at the campground, it was full; however they had an overflow area that was available.

There was a visitor's center nearby, so they decided to check that out. They discovered that each year on the weekend nearest the anniversary of that battle, the Indians had a reenactment of the Battle of the Little Big Horn and Dick and Mary had arrived on that weekend. In fact they had arrived just in time for that evening's reenactment.

The location of the reenactment was some distance out of Harding and was a permanent installation with large amounts of seating where the stage was a rolling knoll in front of the seating. Dick and Mary got there just in time for the evening event.

This production was completely put together by the Indians. In fact the narration was done by an Indian and they suggested that the narration of the battle was done by the only survivors of the battle;

the Indians, as Custer and ALL of his men were annihilated. Another little known fact was discussed. General Custer, two of his brothers, one nephew and one brother-in-law were all killed in the battle, for a total of five Custer's who died as a result of Custer showing the world how to fight Indians.

Their next adventure was taking a ride to an old abandoned mining town by the name of Leadville that is located within the confines of Death Valley, however to get there you first must go into Nevada, then double back into Death Valley from a place called Beatty, Nevada. If you choose to check this place out, it is strongly suggested you do some serious homework first.

Once you find the road and begin your adventure, the first stop is a gate with many signs, because once you pass THAT GATE you are LOCKED into a nearly thirty mile drive with ABSOLUTELY NO CHANCE OF CHANGING YOUR MIND. The first couple of miles are on a reasonably well groomed dirt road, and then the fun begins WHEN ALL HELL BREAKS LOOSE. Incidentally Dick should tell you what he was driving before we go any further. Dick was driving a 1993 Dodge RAM 2400 Diesel truck with four wheel drive, six speed manual transmission and a six foot box. This information is important as you will soon see. The road was originally built for a team of horses and at the very best an average sized wagon. It has been widened slightly since it was built, but there just AIN'T no place to go for you see the left side of the road is a shear wall and the right side of the road is a sheer cliff, with a vertical drop of hundreds of feet in many places. Incidentally, there is virtually no shoulder. Many of the switchbacks are so sharp that one backup was required on numerous occasions, and two were necessary occasionally. They finally got over that mountain and breathed a sigh of relief.

After travelling another mile or two, they came to a second mountain that was just as bad, if not worse than the first. Finally the road came down into a fairly wide valley where the ghost town of Leadville is located. There is not much to see there, but it was a welcome relief from the previous driving. There were a few broken down buildings and they found one abandoned mine shaft.

It was soon time to begin the last half of the journey. The road from Leadville back to Death Valley was completely different from what we had previously seen, by following a deep, narrow canyon all the way to the mouth of the canyon. There were no switch backs and no steep cliffs that they needed to worry about, which sure was a relief; however, the road was full of deep heavy sand and small stones, with a very steep gradient. Even with the steep gradient, Dick needed to drive the truck in second gear and four wheel drive all the way to the exit of the canyon, where upon they came out at the top of a very large alluvial fan or cone.

To give you some idea of the ferocity of some of the water that comes down those canyons, the fan was littered with large rocks, some as large as cars. Seeing that in operation must be a sight to behold.

Incidentally, if you are sure you would like to duplicate this adventure; my recommendation for a vehicle would be a small four wheel drive Jeep.

This next adventure is also in Death Valley and took place in late September; however the year is unknown, and unimportant.

When reaching Death Valley, they entered the park on Route 190, which is the main road that goes East-West across the park.

Almost immediately after entering the park they met several very large snowplows; however there did not appear to be any snow on the ground so we followed those plows for a short distance to see what they were going to plow. Apparently, the day before there had been very heavy storms in the mountains, the same mountains that we had traversed in our previous visit when we visited Leadville. The storms had been so severe that the many canyons had filled with water and washed much mud, sand, stones and boulders down into Death Valley. Those snow plows were simply going to remove all of that debris from the highway. That was the first time Dick had ever seen a snow plow used to move rocks and sand.

There is time for just one more story. The first year that Dick lived in Colorado Springs, one of the first guys that Dick hired was a military transplant from Ohio and he convinced Dick that he should take up skiing since they were now living in true ski country. Following his advice they began skiing at Monarch, located near Salida. They tried skiing and Dick liked it, so it kind of became a standard weekend routine. Since Dick had two cars, he normally drove. They would normally travel south out of Colorado Springs on State Route 115, then turn west on US 50 and straight on to Monarch Ski area. It was on the return trip home one evening that this event took place.

There is a place known as Royal Gorge on US 50 that provides a great place to spend a couple of days with your family. Dick and his wife JoyAnn had spent some time there checking out the sites and entertainment, as well as the rides and numerous other features. First it is home to the world's Highest Suspension bridge over the Arkansas River at a mere 1200 feet. The most interesting part of that bridge is the decking which is made of planking, thus there is a space between each plank, allowing you to look straight down into the river 1200 feet below. Many people find that view very unsettling.

There is other entertainment there which includes a cable tram across the gorge and a cable car to the bottom of the gorge, a small train, plus numerous live animals. In other words it is a great place to take the kids.

They have one other spectacular feature which you don't want to miss. It is a road within a mile or so of US 50 that essentially runs parallel to it for about three miles, known as Skyline Drive, with an eastern terminus in Canon City. Canon City also has a very large State prison that US 50 passes right in front of. So what is the significance you may ask? History tells us that Sky Line drive was built with labor that was provided in the early 1930's by the inmates from that prison.

So what is unique about Sky Line Drive? The road was built right on the crest of a very large Hogs Back Land formation, some 800 feet above US 50 which it parallels. The road is one lane wide with three or four feet extra width. In other words, it is almost exactly one car width wide. All traffic moves one way from west to east. There are numerous pull offs where drivers can stop and regain their composure, and take some outstanding photographs. You also need to give the traffic that is backed up behind you an opportunity to pass. Now for the best part, there are no guard rails, just very steep banks on BOTH sides of the road that you would need ropes to descend or CLIMB in most places.`

Dicks' skiing partner had been living in Colorado for some time but had never heard of this road so Dick suggested that on the return trip from skiing, they take a short detour to check out the scenery. Dick and his wife Joy Ann had gone over the road two or three times, so Dick was prepared for the thrill this time. A word of caution; if any of your passengers have any great fear of height, DO NOT TAKE them on this road. Dick's friend was very happy when this shortcut was over.

As we come to the end of the Louis and Clark story, as well as several additional short stories, there is one more recent story left to tell. As earlier stated Dick had a massive heart attack in 2014, however this story goes back to the 1960's and 1970's time frame. It was during that time frame that Dick and his close friend Doc were doing a lot of backpacking in various Wilderness Areas for relatively extended periods of time. Frequently during those trips they would get into deep philosophical discussions and this trip was no exception. Dick does not remember the precise date, or the particular Wilderness Area, but he does remember the issue. First, Doc was a Physician, specializing in the treatment of cancer patients, thus he made the generalized statement that over the years he had seen many patients come and go. He then went on to talk about the different people and the different ways they handle the ultimate solution, basically death.

He discovered early on in his career that there is basically two ways people approach death. One approach is with much Fear and Anxiety and the other approach is with Grace and Dignity. He further stated that as a young Doc he decided to see if he could determine what caused people to be in one group or the other.

After a long period of observation and study he determined that each group had many common characteristics. Basically, the group that accepted death with Grace and Dignity had lived a very full and satisfying life; they had accomplished all or more than they had ever hoped for, and thus were ready to move on to the next chapter of their being. On the other hand, the other group had accomplished virtually nothing, or at least very little, thus they couldn't leave just yet as they were still waiting for something big to happen.

It is now time for the more recent part of the story. Thursday July 31, 2014 began very much like nearly all Thursdays during the summer months with Dick and Mary driving to Clinton, NY to attend the day long Farmer's Market. This particular day was just the same as many times before with Dick helping Mary set up the market in the morning, then returning home to work on the many tasks that needed his attention there. On a normal day, as it was on this particular day, Dick returned to the Market at about 1600 hours to help Mary pack up the remains of the Market for the return home.

This is the point where the routine began to change. After helping Mary for several minutes Dick began to feel light headed and a bit dizzy where upon he told Mary he needed to sit down for a couple of minutes. Almost immediately after setting down, he began to sweat, profusely. This was the trigger point for Mary to call 911. This call went to the Clinton Volunteer Fire Department, physically located maybe two hundred yards from where Dick was located. Two Firemen and an EMT were in the Firehouse after work getting the place in shipshape. These three men RAN from the Fire House to where Mary was located and arrived even before Mary could hang up the phone. The EMT immediately recognized the symptoms as those of a heart attack and administered the appropriate medications.

While all of that was taking place the Ambulance arrived and Dick was loaded into the Rumble Seat and they started to roll. While all of this activity was taking place the EMT was doing an EKG and coordinating with St Elizabeth Hospital. Suddenly the EMT turned to Dick and stated "this is no joke, you are having a massive heart attack". Almost concurrent with that statement, there was a major shift in the urgency that the ambulance was travelling. So how does the story about the backpack trip relate to Dick?

As they wheeled him off the ambulance at St Elizabeth Hospital and into the catheterization Lab that previous story flashed across his mind. You always wonder how you will react when you are faced with that issue, as you think you know, but you are never really sure until you get to that door. It was total serenity, and extremely peaceful.

While they were performing the procedure, in essence removing the blood clot, Dick had been watching the monitor all the time while lying on his back when suddenly the lights began to fade out. His eyes began to close, his head slowly rolled to the left and down and then there was no more. It was at this time when Dick got a peek at the other side.

After some period of time, only God knows how long, Dick came back to the living and he was talking to the Doctor. The Doctor advised him they were down to the last five minutes when they got him restarted. The Doctor had been talking to the EMT who had ridden with Dick in the ambulance and who told the Doctor the whole story. The Doctor told Dick if the incident had occurred a hundred yards further up the street in Clinton there would have been no more tomorrows.

Another chance encounter with "DESTINY" for without that encounter there would have been NO BOOK, for you see, Dick was only in the hospital for three nights and during one of those nights the duty nurse, after hearing a few stories, convinced Dick that he should write a book about his adventures. That is how it all began.

Photo Collection of Memories

The photo of a 1931 Chevrolet was taken in the mid 1940's (goats and all) around 1945. This car represents the first automobile that Dick has any recollection of, and the barn(s) in the background were also on the Palmer family farm.

This photo captures Dick's first meeting with his friend King after Dick had been stationed at Chanute AFB Illinois while attending Air Weather School. Dick had been gone for about six months. This is one of the few pictures that Dick has of himself in uniform and was taken in September 1955 after he had been in the Air Force for nearly one year.

The *handsome* guy in this photo is Mahlon (Dick) Palmer while stationed at Incurlic Air Force Base in Turkey during 1956/57. Notice he is not in uniform since they were not allowed to wear their uniforms in Turkey except while on duty. Dick would have been about eighteen years old when this photo was taken. The building over his left shoulder was his barracks where he lived for the last five or six months that he was there.

This stone bridge is located in Adana, Turkey and crosses the Seyhan River. It is also the oldest stone bridge in the world that remains in use today, having been built in the 2nd century A.D. A new bridge has been built since Dick was there to handle the more modern and high speed traffic.

Mustafa Kemal Ataturk (19 May 1881 – 10 November 1938) was a Turkish army officer, reformist statesman and the first President of Turkey. He is credited with being the founder of the Republic of Turkey. His surname, Ataturk (meaning "Father of the Turks") was granted to him in 1934 and forbidden to be used by any other person by the Turkish parliament.

In essence, he is to Turkey the same as George Washington is to the United States. Thus there are many monuments and parks named after him. This photo was taken in Ataturk Park in downtown Adana, and is representative of many such parks in Turkey.

St Paul's First Church of Antioch was originally established by Saint Paul and was the place where he systematically began his ministry in probably around the fifth century. The New Testament Book of Acts speaks frequently of this church and of the eventual martyrdom of Saint Paul. Dick Palmer is standing in the main door way into the church. This Church is located in the mountains in the central part of Turkey.

This view of St Paul's first church in Antioch provides a view of the complete front of the church. Notice, it appears to seal up the front of a large cave behind it. There was a large stone alter inside.

Andros Island in the Bahamas is home of a relatively large Navel Test site known as AUTEC (Atlantic Underwater Test and Evaluation Center) where Dick spent a total of about two months while working for RCA. AUTEC had a major impact on Dick's future career while he worked for RCA. The photo is of a Light House near the hotel where he stayed while there.

There were many coconut trees on Andros Island and one day a young native boy told us he could climb a tree and get a coconut for us. After seeing how it was done, Dick decided he would give it a try. As you can see he was successful, thus we had fresh coconuts throughout the remainder of our stay.

The Ballistic Missile Early Warning Site at Clear, Alaska.

This photo clearly shows the three large directional radars that each measure 160 feet tall by 400 feet in length. The site had its own coal fired power plant as seen on the right, with the 160 foot diameter tracking radar visible in the background between the power plant and the first large radar screen in the foreground. The temperature at the time this photo was taken was a balmy 40 degrees below zero. Temperatures of sixty to seventy degrees below zero were relatively common.

A comparable BMEWS (Ballistic Missile Early Warning Site) site is located at the J-Site, some 20-30 miles north of Thule AFB in northern Greenland, only that site had four of the large directional radar screens; otherwise they were nearly the same. One major difference, it usually was not as cold in Greenland as in Alaska; however the winds were much worse in Greenland, many times reaching one hundred knots and many times much above that. In fact the wind and blowing snow could be so severe that you could literally not see your own hand a foot in front of your face.

The C-130 aircraft that is being unloaded is parked in front of the DEW Line site in the background. There are two similar sites on the ice cap in Greenland and this is the southernmost site of the two.

This is Mount McKinley as seen from the pilot's seat while flying north from Anchorage, Alaska to Point Barrow, Alaska (Point Barrow being the most northern point in the continental United States). The aircraft was a standard Fairchild F-227 twin engine plane that was used for the vast majority of our travel. Incidentally, the outline of a face on the right side of the photo is that of the pilot. We were flying at close to 20 thousand feet (20,000) at that time with the height of Mount McKinley at 20,320 feet.

This photo is of Dick practicing his new skill of repelling down a sheer 150 foot wall in Canyonlands NP. The first time or two over the edge is pretty scary; however after that it becomes very addictive.

Major John Wesley Powell's Survey Marker.

At the confluence of the Colorado and Green Rivers is a survey marker placed there by Major John Wesley Powell on one of his expeditions down the Green and Colorado Rivers. The maker is dated around 1900 and we located the marker on one of our backpacking trips into the Maze Section of Canyonlands National Park. The only way the marker could be found at that time was to enter the park on the western edge of the Western section.

The Park (at least at that time) was comprised of three separate sections, with no ability to travel between the sections within the park. There were also no roads within the Maze Section at that time.

This is the actual inscription on the Powell Survey Marker. Much of the marker has weathered away over time, thus it is difficult to read.

Dick and his Service Dog Bramble (In Training) are participating in Armed Forces Day activities on behalf of the Civil Air Patrol. Dick's friend, Barbara made this uniform for Bramble plus many more costumes for other occasions.

During the time when Dick had his airplane he was a very active member of the Utica-Rome Civil Air Patrol. Not only was there much flying involved but also a significant amount of participation in civil events such as Parades and Armed Forces Days, etc. As a result, Dick took it upon himself to build a float for use in those events. This float was built on an old lawnmower for the frame and he must admit it was very well received in the parades. Notice the pilot in this particular photo is one of Dick's trained Service Dogs named Bramble.

Dick purchased this airplane shortly after receiving his pilot's
license. It was a 1965 Piper Cherokee Model PA-28, with 180
horsepower engine. He owned this aircraft for just over twenty
years at which time he decided to sell due to excessive "Old Timer's"
insurance rates and other maintenance costs. Dick and his very
good friend Barbara Putt have just returned from a joyride to the
Albany area where they had breakfast.

Delicate Arch as seen through another arch in Arches National Park. The name of the Arch in the foreground has been lost to the ages.

There is a story in the main text that describes the hike that resulted in this photograph of Apikuni Falls in Glacier National Park. The falls have an estimated height of about 150 feet.

The geyser that is erupting in the background is the world famous Old Faithful in Yellowstone National Park as a buffalo enjoys his lunch in the foreground. Check the main text for the rest of this story as you might find it somewhat unusual. The probability of getting this photograph under these circumstances was astronomical.

This photo shows a large area being prepared to remove the overburden from a large open pit coal mine in New Mexico. The long rows identify the location where the explosives have been 'planted' in preparation for the blast. Once the area is prepared and the explosives are in place, the entire area is blasted. The blast begins at one edge, and then moves progressively across the entire field; however the sequence is accomplished in milliseconds, thus the appearance is one big blast.

After the explosives were all in place and everyone was at least one-half mile away, it was time to detonate the field. Each explosive charge was detonated 1/100th of a second after the previous blast, giving the illusion of a single blast. The blast was not designed to be spectacular, but rather to shatter the overburden so that it could be removed with gigantic dragline buckets, making the coal below accessible for strip mining.

The Black Canyon of the Gunnison is a National Park located in western Colorado, having become a National Park in 1999. This very unusual wall is located in the Black Canyon of the Gunnison on the north wall. This wall is called the Painted Wall and is the tallest sheer cliff in Colorado at 2,250 feet. The lighter striations are made of pegmatite. The Gunnison River drops an average of 34 feet per mile through the entire canyon, making it the fifth steepest descent in North America.

Cris Lewis-Artist

Cris Lewis completed a thirty year career teaching in a Career Tech school in Central New York. After attending a watercolor art show, watercolor painting went on her list of to do's in retirement. A hobby became a career.

A few months into retirement a cancer diagnosis turned into getting a Cavalier King Charles Spaniel puppy, Murphy. Her first portrait was of Murphy in a Christmas portrait/card. As a result, painting pets and other animals is her passion. She has completed numerous commissions. Her work has received ribbons at the New York State Fair and Rome Art Association Show. She has had multimedia solo shows. She also enjoys Chinese watercolor, landscapes and quilting. Much of her artwork is influenced by her travels throughout the US visiting her children, as well as travel to China with international artist Lian Zhen.

Cris has studied at Munson William Proctor Institute and Kirkland Art Center with Ralph Murray, Jane Grace Taylor and Kathy Kernan.

Her work may be seen and purchased at Artisans' Corner, in Clinton, NY.